MORAL TALES

Portrait of Jules Laforgue by Franz Skarbina, 1885

Jules Laforgue

MORAL TALES

TRANSLATED WITH AN INTRODUCTION BY
WILLIAM JAY SMITH

A NEW DIRECTIONS BOOK

The preparation of this volume was made possible, in part, by a grant from
the Program for Translations of the National Endowment for the Humani-
ties, an independent Federal agency.

The translations of "Hamlet" and "The Miracles of the Roses" appeared
in *Selected Writings of Jules Laforgue*, edited and translated by William
Jay Smith (Grove Press, 1956); the translations of "Perseus and Andromeda" and "Lohengrin" appeared in *Translation*, vol. II, 1974, and
vol. XII, 1984; and a section of the introduction appeared in *Jules Laforgue:
Essays on a Poet's Life and Work*, edited by Warren Ramsey, with a
preface by Harry T. Moore (Southern Illinois University Press, 1964).

This translation is based on Daniel Grojnowski's critical edition of
Moralités légendaires, published in 1980 by Librairie Droz (Paris-Geneva).
Thanks are due the editor and publisher for use of their text.

Manufactured in the United States of America
First published clothbound and as New Directions Paperbook 594 in 1985
Published simultaneously in Canada by Penguin Books Canada Limited

Library of Congress Cataloging in Publication Data

Laforgue, Jules, 1860–1887.
    Moral tales.
    (A New Directions Book)
    Translation of: Moralités légendaires.
    1. Parodies—Translations from French.
2. Parodies, French—Translations into English.
I. Title.
PQ2323.L8M613 1985   841'.8   84-25498
ISBN 0-8112-0942-3
ISBN 0-8112-0943-1 (pbk.)

New Directions Books are published for James Laughlin
by New Directions Publishing Corporation,
80 Eighth Avenue, New York 10011

This translation is dedicated

to

DAVID ARKELL

my friend and Laforgue's

CONTENTS

INTRODUCTION

When early one November morning in 1881, Jules Laforgue left Paris by the Gare de l'Est to join the German court in Coblenz and take up his position as French reader to the seventy-year-old Empress Augusta, he was an intelligent, inexperienced, and unformed young man of twenty-one: he was traveling, as he expressed it, "into a great dream." A dream it was, the ordered, artificial life he led in Berlin, Baden-Baden, and Coblenz, reading daily from French books and newspapers of the time to that descendant of Catherine the Great of Russia who was such a Francophile that she refused to tolerate a word of German in her presence. But throughout the dream the dreamer's eyes were open and attentive, capable of creating what Laforgue called those "lightning flashes of identity between subject and object—the attribute of genius." The man who returned to Paris five years later possessed an extraordinary maturity of mind and had produced imaginative works whose importance would grow with time.

On 30 December 1886 the poet traveled to London, where the next day he married Leah Lee, the pretty young English woman with whom he had studied English in Berlin. On their return to Paris early in January, his health deteriorated rapidly; he died of tuberculosis on 20 August 1887, four days after his twenty-seventh birthday. His wife died of the same disease ten months later.

Laforgue's life was tragically brief but immensely productive: he would be remembered by generations of writers in Europe and America: many would look on him as the most gifted of the Symbolists. An accomplished ironist, Laforgue succeeded for the first time in bringing all the machinery, the shabby and sordid décor of modern life, into poetry. He was compelled to make poetry out of everything, omitting, as Arthur Symons pointed out, no hour of the day or night. It was through Symons that

T. S. Eliot discovered Laforgue, and the ironic framework and often the actual words of much of Eliot's early poetry owe everything to him. Influenced to some degree by Whitman, some of whose poems he translated, Laforgue made the first effective use of *vers libre*. In his "Hamlet," as well as in his *Derniers Vers*, Laforgue experimented with a stream-of-consciousness technique that was to be continued by Edouard Dujardin and James Joyce. Laforgue's verbal experiments were in many ways similar to the visual experiments of the Impressionists. His pioneering essay on Impressionism remains one of the most judicious appraisals of the movement. He also left behind a spirited book on Berlin and the German court. The descriptions and impressions of the natural scene in his notebooks call to mind the inscapes of Gerard Manley Hopkins or the poems of Elizabeth Bishop. And the freshness and charm of his letters have prompted some critics to refer to him as the French Keats. No work shows more completely the range of his youthful genius than his *Moralités légendaires*, completed shortly before his death. Mallarmé called them the tales of Symbolism that Voltaire might have written.

—— II ——

"Jules Laforgue—what joy!" said his contemporary J. K. Huysmans, and nowhere in all his work does one feel the aptness of this remark more than in his *Moral Tales*. Here, as in his final poems, Laforgue is at the height of his inventive powers. What delight there is in these exquisitely wrought tales; what flash and sparkle of genius. There is surely no prose of the late nineteenth century that is so ornate without being heavy: it is light to the occasional point of frivolity but somehow always firm; it is delicate but rarely weak. Here Laforgue works within the fullness of his orbit, and only on the sure base of sensibility could rise such intaglio of intellect. "From the sublime to the arabesque," James Gibbons Huneker said of Laforgue, "is but a semitone in his antic mood." And so in these tales he moves, giving dimension with a quick brush-stroke to everyday events and objects, making what is ordinary and everyday seem fantastical and strange, and what is strange and fantastical ordinary and everyday. While Perseus rides off through the air to return to the "pays élégants et faciles," Andromeda remains with the Dragon on the "pauvre île quotidienne." And the reader knows that she is right to remain: the Monster, after all, is a good friend, gentleman, poet, and scholar, who will spend hours polishing pebbles for her in much the way that Spinoza polished his lenses. That he becomes transformed immediately into a prince is but the final triumph of her accommodation to her routine day-to-day existence with him.

At first glance, Laforgue's purpose in the *Moralités légendaires* appears to be a stylistic one: he wishes to dispense with bombast and grandiloquence, to restore to art a sense of proportion and common sense, to wring the neck of rhetoric in his own way. But as in all his work, this stylistic purpose reflects a deeper psychological one. He began to write these tales, which he called originally *Petites moralités légendaires*, in the fall of 1883, the first one being "The Miracle of the Roses." The stories are, in a sense, a parallel development to the *Complaintes*. In the poems he attempted to cast traditional poetic and philosophical themes in common everyday popular songs; in the stories, he brings myth and lofty legend down to earth, he cuts his heroes down to size. Of course, the simplest and most direct, if not always the most effective, means of accomplishing this is through parody; indeed, the *Moralités* have been called nothing but "parodies artificielles." It is true that, at their worst, they do degenerate into a kind of schoolboy burlesque, as at times in "Salome." The wit disintegrates in places, and we have a sense of the smart aleck; something gets between the author and his material, and the result is a series of monkeyshines. Even at his worst, however, Laforgue is never gross nor uncouth; the comedy almost always remains that of the drawing room rather than of the smoking car. But parody is not Laforgue's real purpose. The *Moralités* seem to point up no moral. In the brief epilogue to "Perseus and Andromeda," the princess who has listened to the tale exclaims to the raconteur: "But it's impossible to discuss anything properly with you, or to learn anything from you. Let's go in and have tea. And, by the way, what is the moral of the story; I always forget the moral?" Laforgue would have us forget the point, for the point is always made by indirection. The moral is as much in how the thing is said as it is in what is said. And what he says in the entire book is that all the past—history, myth, and legend—exists everywhere and for all of us: we are in it, and it is in us.

The past is a living thing, and our heroes are where we find them. Perseus, alighting from his hippogriff, might have just arrived by taxi for the *bal des quat'z-arts:*

> Perseus wears the helmet of Pluto that renders its wearer invisible; his arms and ankles bear the wings of Mercury, and he carries the divine shield of Pallas Athena. From his belt swings the head of the Gorgon Medusa whose single glance changed the giant Atlas, as we all know, into a mountain, and his hippogriff is Pegasus, which was ridden by Bellerophon when he slew the Chimera. This young hero looks extremely sure of himself.

We know exactly what to expect of him. Lohengrin appears on his taciturn, heraldic swan, "glissant, grandissant, magique, gardant sa pose, sûr de tout!" He is the essence of refinement and polish, this "jeune homme de Diane," but he is also most ineffectual; and we are not astonished when in the Nuptial Villa his pillow is transformed into a swan and he is carried back to his heavenly home. Hamlet is presented as a little creature so unimposing physically that he is scarcely even recognized at Elsinore as a royal personage.

"Poor humanity has not produced a *pure hero*," Laforgue wrote, "and all those that are cited to us in antiquity are creatures like ourselves who have been crystallized in legend—neither

Buddha, Socrates, nor Marcus Aurelius—I'd like to know their daily lives." Laforgue always had his personal and private reasons for depicting his heroes as he did: indeed, he put a great deal that is recognizably himself into his "Hamlet."

Hamlet was for Laforgue, as G. Jean-Aubry pointed out, what St. Anthony was for Flaubert: no character of legend or literature so haunted his imagination. Laforgue's tale gives a double image: it is Hamlet seeing himself as Hamlet, or rather, since the work in this case is so clearly personal, it is Laforgue as Hamlet seeing himself as Hamlet. The poet is concerned specifically with only two scenes from the original drama: the play and the graveyard scene. Beginning in the middle and going to the heart of the matter, he gives us the play within the play. One might say that he had attempted to outline the background that is essential to a full understanding of the tragedy. What appear to be the least significant aspects for Shakespeare become the hard core for Laforgue: his work is an essay in indirection, a playful criticism transcending parody. One of the early reviewers of the *Moralités* stated with justice that Laforgue had reduced a fresco to a drawing while retaining the masterful line. He manages to do so, I think, not by copying the whole but by concentrating on certain details that only the most careful and experienced viewer can detect. Max Beerbohm once said that he thought that the scene with Yorick's skull would have been more effective if Shakespeare had given us an example of how the fool once entertained the royal table. This Laforgue has done; for he has written, as he expressed it, *à la Yorick,* combining hero and fool. How explain Hamlet's madness? Quite simply: he is Yorick's brother—they had the same gypsy mother. And like Yorick, he is an actor, but an actor who is overwhelmed by his rôle, an artist who becomes enamored of his creation. When Kate recites his lines and he sees his creation come to life before his eyes, it is too much for him. This is a case of "Galatea blinding Pygmalion," as Laforgue wrote elsewhere. Hamlet is a dilettante philosopher for whom there is "life and life's surrounding territory, with a great deal of glorious pessimism thrown in." Laforgue made several sketches of the body of a dandy with top hat and cane in hand, surmounted by a death's-head. Here, in Hamlet, he has created the same "hollow man." He has put Yorick's skull on the Prince's shoulders, and the effect is bizarre but powerful.

Laforgue created the Hamlet of the twentieth century, a Hamlet whose mock-seriousness has become today's current coin. The young pale-faced dandy who carries a cane rather than a sword and seems to have nothing on his mind because he has so much is familiar to us all, and his disturbing laughter is still heard.

Although his heroes are at times rather hopelessly immature, they are, for all their posturing, ordinary people. In the destruction of the hero there is still something heroic that survives. With this treatment of myth, Laforgue, poetically and intuitively, hit upon a wholly modern approach; the heroes of the past must be recreated by each human consciousness in its own way; they are perpetually waiting to be reborn. It is this perception, which psychologically and artistically places Laforgue far in advance of his time, that interested James Joyce. (And we know from Padraic Colum that Joyce admired the tales early in his career.) Without Laforgue's *Moral Tales* Joyce's *Ulysses* would not have been possible.

The pages of these stories are marked by constant references to the Unconscious, which became a focal point for Laforgue's very personal aesthetic principles. No single book was as important to Laforgue as Eduard von Hartmann's *Philosophy of the Unconscious*, which appeared in French translation in 1877. Reacting against positivism, Hartmann saw the world as governed by an all-powerful unconscious spirit, subject to no influence. Laforgue made use of this metaphysical principle for his own artistic purposes. Like the Imagination for Wallace Stevens, it became for Laforgue the one real good, the "necessary angel." "The Unconscious blows where it listeth," he wrote, "let it do just that and our arts will follow . . . Its principle is the anarchy of life: let it lead us where it may, let us delight in the limitless treasures of our senses." Laforgue summed up his new-found artistic freedom with the battle cry:

Aux armes, citoyens, il n'y a plus de RAISON.

To arms, citizens, REASON is dead.

The cry would become the rallying point for the Surrealists.

In his artistic interpretation of the Unconscious, Laforgue sounds often as if he is speaking of the Negative Capability of Keats. In his essay on Impressionism, he says: "Each man, according to his moment in time, his race and social condition, his personal stage of development, is a keyboard on which the exterior world plays in a particular way . . . My keyboard is perpetually changing and there is not another exactly like mine. All keyboards are legitimate."

So completely did Laforgue live through his eyes that one can almost say that he saw these tales as tone poems and assigned to each of them a certain color: black to "Hamlet," red to "The Miracle of the Roses," white to "Lohengrin," yellow to "Salome," green and gold to "Pan and the Syrinx," gray to "Perseus and Andromeda," and violet to "The Two Pigeons," which Laforgue decided to eliminate from the book. Each story is bathed in its own color; and the reader has the sense as he proceeds of experiencing an entire scale of color values. The "Lohengrin" of Laforgue with its ice-cold lunar landscape bears many resemblances to "The Eve of St. Agnes" of Keats, and like Keats, Laforgue is aware of the emotional overtones which color can provide. The descriptive passages in the *Moralités légendaires* do not exist apart from the story; the detail, exquisite in itself, serves to move the plot forward. The landscape, in some remarkable way, actually helps to define the characters; as in a finely wrought tapestry, all is interwoven with extreme care. Salome, in her spidery jonquil chiffon with its black polka dots, has a real affinity with the heavens; she is actually a manifestation of the Moon Goddess, an earthly projection of the Milky Way.

Two themes are paramount in all the tales: one is the proximity of death ("Adieu paniers, vendanges sont faites!"), the other, the permanence of art ("Vous voyez bien, vous-même; il n'y a que l'art; l'art c'est le désir perpétué"). Perhaps it is Laforgue's youth and his awareness of an early death, as well as of his own genius, that gives the tales, like the best of his poems, their special poignancy. The turning point of "Lohengrin" comes when the Knight-Errant turns to Elsa and says, as he caresses her in a curious, abstracted way: "Cette Villa-Nuptiale sent la fosse commune," and Elsa replies, "Nous sommes tous mortels." The grave gapes wherever Laforgue looks, and it is always attended by the beautiful goddess, Our Lady the Moon, the Moon Goddess, Death-in-Life, *la belle dame sans merci*. Ruth, the consumptive heroine of "The Miracle of the Roses," wears on her breast a strange enamel medallion around which the story revolves; this medallion represents the spot of a peacock's tail resting under a human eyelid. It is thus a symbolical presentation of the Evil Eye which is inevitably linked with death: in its core of purple, it signifies here the dark of the moon. The story may be said to relate, therefore, a lunar eclipse: the Holy Sacrament representing the male symbol, the Sun, passes before the female, the Moon; and a miracle is accomplished in the brief meeting of life and death. The continued spilling of blood throughout the story has furthermore quite clear sexual connotations; in the blood of the female there is life and death. Laforgue says elsewhere:

> *La Femme?*
> *—J'en sors,*
> *La mort*
> *Dans l'âme . . .*

As for Woman—
I come from her womb,
My eyes fixed
Upon my tomb.

But also attendant at the grave throughout is the artist. Hamlet is above all else an artist, a poet who seems more interested in the success of his play than in justice or revenge, and as an artist he dies: "Qualis . . . artifex . . . pereo." In "Pan and the Syrinx," one of the most beautiful of the tales, the nymph is "perpetuated" on the reed flute of Pan: art is triumphant. "Pan and the Syrinx" and "Perseus and Andromeda" appear to have been written in 1886 and 1887 after Laforgue's courtship and marriage; and both stories are more luminous, more affirmative than any Laforgue had written previously.

Laforgue was always falling in love with the same woman, and she seemed always to have the traits of Leah Lee, his future wife, as he described her to his sister: "She's as tall as you or I, but very thin and very English, decidedly English, with her reddish brown hair, a red you simply can't imagine and one I would never have believed existed until I saw her, pale skin, thin neck and eyes, those eyes, you must see them." The heroines of the *Moral Tales*, from Kate in "Hamlet" right through to Andromeda and the Syrinx are all the same. Laforgue's visits to the prostitutes of the Friedrichstrasse in Berlin made him long for pure young girls, preferably English ones since they seemed the purest. Laforgue said at one point that there are three sexes, men, women, and English girls; and he wanted English girls. "But the pure young girls were just not available," David Arkell points out, "at least not to Laforgue. Time after time he would beg them (in his notes) to come off their pedestals and mend their mincing ways, but they always failed to get the message. Finally he decided it was neither his fault nor theirs—their regrettable behavior had simply been imprinted in them at birth. And at this point he comes so near to the ideas of today's Women's Movement that he has been hailed as an ally by no less person than Simone de Beauvoir. 'In all his work,' she says in *Le Deuxième Sexe* (1949), 'Laforgue expressed his rancor against the mystification [of women] for which he held men as responsible as women.'" Laforgue admired Leah Lee not just for her beauty but also for her independence: by living and traveling alone, she showed herself to be a free woman, no longer bound by the strict moral code imposed by a male-dominated society.

Laforgue, the writer, like Laforgue, the artist, was more and more attached to life the nearer he came to death. The Medusa's deadly eyes close when confronted with the Dragon in "Perseus and Andromeda": the Medusa cannot harm an old friend. Laforgue wanted to believe that the goddess could be kind, but even in the few glorious golden days he experienced before his death—that period of elation and heightened vision so familiar to the consumptive—he was not wholly convinced: he knew that she was more often cruel. And indeed she was. But the goddess who demanded his life was also his muse, and no matter how exacting her demands, in the end he had served her well.

"A little more piety!" Laforgue exclaimed at one point. "Art is not just a schoolboy's exercise, *it is all of life*." Art *was* life to Laforgue, and he left no better testimonial to the fact than his *Moral Tales*. Art for art's sake, yes, which meant art for life's sake as well. And how paradoxical it is that there can be so much life in a book so concerned with death, and so much freshness of spirit in a work so artificial in nature. In the notebook Laforgue kept in Berlin in 1884–85, he remarks that formerly he had seen only things themselves, but that now he had begun to see the shadows of things. The shadows are present here in the *Moralités*, and they would surely have lengthened with time.

—— III ——

In England at the end of the nineteenth century, as Louise Bogan pointed out, the ruling taste had created numerous objects that threatened to smother the very public for which they were designed and the expression of open eroticism was banned on all sides. It was at this point that Beardsley, she writes, "with his sinister rococo line shows up every detail of that taste—basic material as well as superimposed pattern, plush and ormolu as well as quilting, puff, tassel, and gilded distortion—and fills this surrounding décor with creatures openly embodying a fantastic, perverse, and deliquescent eroticism, whose disabused eyes look out on a sort of dressmakers' and upholsterers' hell. This is the terror of the end-of-the-century vision at its highest point; and this sort of vision could not be driven underground, we now realize, entirely, or for long."

This vision forms the very basis of Laforgue's tales. Laforgue deals with social and literary poses, outmoded forms of expression and attitude; and, as Ezra Pound put it, "makes them a vehicle for the expression of his own very personal emotions, of his own unperturbed sincerity." He was, Pound says, "a purge and a critic": "He laughed out the errors of Flaubert, i.e., the clogging and cumbrous historical detail. He left *Coeur Simple, L'Education, Madame Bovary, Bouvard*. His *Salomé* makes game of the rest."

Laforgue attempted in his *Moral Tales*, as in his *Derniers Vers*, to break down all barriers, to attain that effect of spontaneity, that "unwritten" quality that we associate with his name. "The only remedy is to break everything," Laforgue wrote. In his tales, as in his last poems, he piles up objects, old newspapers, soiled linen, fashion plates, everyday banal things alongside sentimental and romantic ones; it is as if a glass bell had shattered and tumbled its ornate flowers, shells, and mementos on the floor: the romantic pile is split apart, revealing the sorry framework, the pathetic assembly, beneath.

Laforgue plays with language as did Edward Lear and Lewis

Carroll. He was an admirer of Kate Greenaway and Randolph Caldecott, and although he never mentions Edward Lear, he may well have admired Lear's nonsense verses and his drawings for children. He would surely have delighted in Lear's verbal inventions such as "plumdomphious," "sponge-taneously," and "scroobious." It is hard to believe that Laforgue's "classic retreat of the Sun" in "Perseus and Andromeda" was not inspired by Edward Lear's description of the "co-operative Cauliflour" in his nonsense tale of the four little children who went round the world. Laforgue's Red Eminence "in his cassock of collapse . . . completely mottled by atrabilious stigmata" is finally kicked over, "a shrunken pumpkinhead." Lear's Cauliflour, supported by "two superincumbent confidential cucumbers" disappears "on the brink of the western sky in a crystal cloud of sudorific sand." Laforgue's *citrouille crevée* is certainly similar to Lear's pumpkin, "quite full of lucifer matches," that subsequently explodes "surreptitiously into a thousand bits." Lear and Laforgue, in their different ways, were revolting against the poetic eloquence of their day, an eloquence of which at the same time they had a great appreciation. Laforgue admired the poems of Hugo; Lear wept on hearing the lyrics of Tennyson. But where Lear's playful language is addressed to children, Laforgue's is directed to the most sophisticated of adult readers.

Laforgue, in his verbal mastery, resembles the young skater whom he describes in "Salome:"

> Attendants then brought in a platform of real ice: a teenage skater sprang forth upon it, arms crossed over the white astrakhan frogging on his chest, and he did not stop until he had executed all known combinations of curves. He waltzed on his toes like a ballerina; etched on the ice a flamboyant Gothic cathedral, without omitting a single rose-window or delicate carved detail; danced a three-part fugue, ending in a whirlwind as inextricable as that of a fakir possessed *del diavolo*, and then left the stage, feet in the air, skating off on fingernails of steel . . .

Like the skater the poet executes every known combination of verbal curves. From invented words coupled with learned and scientific expressions, he moves to literary and historical allusions, purposely mangled folk sayings and ribald puns. He breaks up delicate poetic language with colloquial phrases from the lowest social milieu. He moves from the sublime to the ridiculous and back again often within a single sentence, always keeping his perfect balance. And while playing verbally with false sentiment, he conveys true feeling. Even when he moves in a straightforward manner as in "Pan and the Syrinx" he is never as simple as he seems. The surface is deceptive; true complexity lies beneath.

These verbal pyrotechnics, dazzling in the original, are the translator's nightmare. If I had set out to annotate these tales completely, my footnotes would have outweighed the text a hundred times. And so I have dispensed with footnotes entirely: an annotated version would be a hodge-podge just as a word-for-word transliteration would be impenetrable nonsense. The line between Laforgue's prose and his poetry is always thin: the storyteller is constantly breaking off into verse or song. To give a sense of this breathless quality, I have kept the direct apostrophes, as strange as they sometimes seem. In translating Laforgue, one must be prepared in every sentence to make both sacrifices and choices. To keep the elegant balance as well as the quick pace of the original, I have made what I hope are the right ones.

Frances Newman, the Atlanta-born author of an interesting experimental novel, *The Hard-Boiled Virgin* (1926), made a valiant attempt to translate these tales, but her *Six Moral Tales from Jules Laforgue*, published in 1928 after her death, is marred by incredible howlers in almost every paragraph. She dedicated her book "to the moonlit memory of Jules Laforgue," and had it bound in Laforgue's "deep-mourning violet." She herself dressed in shades of violet and wrote always on yellow paper.

In the last year of her life, she went to France to complete her translation of the *Moral Tales*. It was a tribute to her talent that her translation received high praise from reviewers, but it was clear that few of them had looked at her text alongside the original. In her version the howlers add at times a surrealist touch that is truly Laforguian, at others, they make for pure silliness. She has the seagulls in "Lohengrin" "proceed to the little sin suitable for fine evenings" instead of having them "go fishing" (*à leur petite pêche*). Hamlet's timid eyes "glisten thoughtfully, and as clearly as water unconcealed by a vase" instead of radiating "limpid and unmuddied thought" (*sans vase*). In "Salome" she has the city "calming itself with soaring irrigations" instead of "drying after a heavy sprinkling" (*essorant ces copieux arrosages*). In "Pan and the Syrinx" Diana's hounds (*molosses*) become her bats and a lecherous Caliban (*luxurieux*) becomes "a rather elegant" one. Syntax as well as vocabulary causes her problems. In "Salome" when boys are chasing dogs along the beach, she has the boys rather than the dogs barking. The result is, to say the least, bizarre.

Ezra Pound, who understood Laforgue better than anyone else, called Laforgue the master of *logopoeia*, "the dance of the intellect among words." "*Logopoeia* does not translate," he said, "but having determined the original author's state of mind you may or may not be able to find a derivative or an equivalent." Pound called his version of Laforgue's "Salome," which he entitled "Our Tetrarchal Précieuse," a "divagation from Jules Laforgue." He published it first in 1918 and subsequently reprinted it in *Pavannes and Divisions*. Pound certainly catches the spirit of the original, but at times his dictionary betrays him into surrealist touches not far from Frances Newman's, as when he has the "chirping of choral societies" (*orphéons*) instead of "bands playing." He also omits one of the main points of Laforgue's story, which is that Iaokanann pays with his head for having taken Salome's virginity.

—— IV ——

As an undergraduate fifty years ago, I began to read Jules Laforgue and almost at once attempted to put some of his poetry and prose into English. Through a curious set of circumstances, I read Laforgue before I read Eliot, and the French poet's light touch has remained a constant inspiration in my own work. Thus, in a very real sense, this translation of Laforgue's *Moral Tales* is the work of nearly half a century. In my *Selected Writings of Jules Laforgue* (1956) I published translations of "Hamlet" and "The Miracle of the Roses." Both have now been considerably revised.

For valuable aid in the early years of my study I am indebted to the late Isabelle de Wyzewa, the daughter of Laforgue's friend Teodor de Wyzewa, from whom I acquired Laforgue's *Notebook 1884–85*, which I later presented to the Library of Congress and from which the unpublished drawings in this volume are taken. For early assistance and encouragement I am also indebted to Barbara Howes, Professor Warren Ramsey, Professor Wallace Fowlie, M. Maurice Dumoncel, and to the late M. G. Jean-Aubry and Dr. Enid Starkie as well as to my co-editor of the journal *Translation*, the late Robert Payne.

For more recent assistance I wish to thank the editors of Laforgue's *Oeuvres complètes*, Daniel Grojnowski, Pierre-Olivier Walzer, Jean-Louis Debauve, and David Arkell. The latter, to whom this volume is dedicated, read through my completed versions of the tales and made many splendid suggestions; his informal biography *Looking for Laforgue* (1979) has also been a great help. I am particularly grateful to Daniel Grojnowski, whose critical edition of *Moralités légendaires*, based on all existing manuscripts, has incorporated important changes. His text, which I have followed, has permitted me to make numerous corrections in my previously published versions. (I have followed the order of the tales in his edition, beginning with Hamlet, a creator, and ending with Pan, another creator, since this is what Laforgue wished.) I am grateful also to M. Jean-Louis Debauve, the author of *Laforgue en son temps* (1972), who spent several hours showing me the poet's unpublished manuscripts in his possession. I wish as well to thank Mr. Marvyn Carton and his daughter Dana Carton Caprio for allowing me to examine the manuscripts of "Le Miracles des roses," "Lohengrin," and "Salomé."

But as valuable as the assistance of all these editors, scholars, collectors, and friends has been, my greatest debt is to another translator, my wife Sonja Haussmann Smith, who shares my admiration for Laforgue and who has brought her knowledge of English, as well as of her native French, to bear on these pages for many years. The solutions to many of the most difficult passages are hers. For any errors remaining I am solely responsible.

January 1985   William Jay Smith

MORAL TALES

To Teodor de Wyzewa

The Queen of Sheba to Saint Anthony: "Laugh then, good hermit! Laugh—I am very gay, as you will see. I pluck my lyre, I dance like a butterfly and I know a host of tales to tell you, one more entertaining than the next."

—Gustave Flaubert

HAMLET
or the Consequences of Filial Piety

When the inclination took him, Hamlet, that odd character, could lean from his favorite window with its thin yellow panes quavering in their leaded lozenges, and make ripples in the water below: in the water, or rather, in the sky reflected in the water. And this was the starting point of his meditations and his aberrations.

The tower, which since his father's irregular decease, had been the absolute abode of the young prince, rises like some forgotten leprous sentinel deep in the royal park, beside the sea that belongs to all. This section of the park is a dumping ground for withered flowers from the royal conservatories, the seedy bouquets of ephemeral festivities. The sea is the Sund, with waves as unreliable as any; beyond, one can see the Norwegian coast and the city of Helsingborg, nesting-place of the indigent and practical-minded Prince Fortinbras.

The base of the tower in which the young and unfortunate prince has settled down once and for all lies rotting away on the edge of a stagnant inlet in which the Sund itself has settled, piling up moldy froth from the tag-ends of its daily impersonal labors.

O poor stagnant inlet! The flotillas of haughty royal swans hardly ever call at its ports. From the grass-choked muddy depths there rise, through rainy twilights, toward the window of this most human prince, the chorale of ancient families of frogs, the slimy rattle discharged by aged cold sufferers whose rheumatic pains and glutinous eggs are unsettled by the slightest atmospheric variation. And the currents set in motion by the laboring boats and the steady downpour of rain have but scant effect on the diseased skin of this bit of aged water, oxydized by a drivel of gall swept across it like liquid malachite, poulticed here and there with groups of flat heart-shaped leaves surrounding rudimentary yellow tulips, bristling with lean bouquets of flowering rushes, and frail umbellate clusters, which look, one might say in passing, like the flowers of our own common carrot.

Oh, poor inlet! Home of the frog and the unconscious blossom! And poor strip of park with those bouquets abandoned by young ladies when midnight sounded. And poor Sund—waves worn out by the inconstant southern winds, nostalgias bounded by the materialistic and everyday establishments of Fortinbras across the way! . . .

That is why, except when broken by storms, this water is indeed a mirror for the unfortunate Prince Hamlet in his outcast tower, in his room with its two yellow windows, one opening on the soiled gray heavens, the broad sea, and the futility of existence, the other on the perpetual lamentation of the wind in the tall trees of the park. Poor room shaking thus in the heart of incurable, insolvent autumn! Shaking even in July, like today. And today is July 14, 1601, a Saturday; and tomorrow is Sunday: and all over the world little girls will make their innocent way to mass.

On the walls, a dozen views of Jutland, paintings of an impeccable naïveté, commissioned some time ago from a painter in irons; a like number adorns every room in the castle. Between the windows, two full-length portraits: one of Hamlet as a dandy, thumb tucked in his rawhide belt, his fetching smile emerging from the sulfurous shadows; the other of his father with roguish, faunlike eyes bedecked in shining new armor, his late father, King Horwendill irregularly deceased in a state of mortal sin—may the Lord protect his soul in accordance with His well-known mercy. On a table, in the insomniac light of the yellow windows, an etcher's plates irremediably eaten away by the filth of leisure hours. A dunghill of books, a small organ, a full-length mirror, a chaise longue, a secret cupboard. (Since his father's ambiguous decease, Hamlet is afraid of being poisoned.) In the bedroom next to the bed, a Gothic structure of wrought iron from which a set of keys can summon forth two wax statuettes, one of Gerutha, Hamlet's mother, and the other of her present husband, the adulterous and fratricidal Fengo, both modeled by a hand fraught with revengeful fancy, their hearts childishly pierced by a needle —and much good may it do them! In the rear of the alcove, alas, a shower.

Dressed in black and wearing his sleepwalker's sombrero, with his dagger at his hip, Hamlet leans on one elbow watching the Sund, the wide and toiling Sund as it stirs up its usual quota of waves, waves that must await the wind so they may romp to their full with the poor fishing boats, the only semblance of expression which brooding fatality permits them.

Between yesterday's sky and tomorrow's yet to come, today's is heavy and dull, hardly relieved, one would say, by the recent cloudburst, but offering the prospect of a fine Sunday tomorrow. And it is already twilight; one of those twilights described with so much feeling by the chroniclers of the time, and the market-day noises of the city of Elsinore are either drowned or diverted toward the taverns, across the wide reservoir that separates the city from the royal domains.

"Ah, would but my life roll out as easy and wide as the waves," sighs Hamlet. "Ah, just to pass from the sea to the clouds, and back again from the clouds to the sea; and let the rest take care of itself!"

And embracing the happy, unconscious panorama with a gesture *ad hoc*, he digresses thus:

"Ah, if I could just force myself to take the trouble! . . . But time is so rich with minutes and so fleeting! And the only sensible thing one can do is keep quiet, keep quiet, and act in consequence. . . Stability, stability, thy name is Woman. . . To be— well, to be if one must. But to be a hero! To begin life already domesticated by time and place, is that the proper struggle for a hero? . . . To be a hero! To have the whole play to myself and reduce the rest of life to a little curtain raiser! . . . If I were a fine young lady, only the lips of a pure hero would awaken my destiny, a hero whose great deeds and mottoes could be cited at the drop of a hat. . . Ah, in this time of *danno* and *vergogna*, as Michelangelo (a man far superior to all our Thorwaldsens) put it, there are no longer any fine young ladies; they have all taken up nursing. All but the little dolls that are so lovely, but alas, so unbreakable, all but the vipers and the little geese whose down makes such pleasant pillows. . . Or not to live as a hero, but just to live! Method, method, what dost Thou want of me? Thou knowest well that I have eaten the fruit of the Unconscious! Thou knowest well that it is I who bring the new law to man who is born of Woman, it is I whose business it is to unseat the Categorical, and install in its place the Climacteric, Imperative."

Prince Hamlet has more of all this on his mind, more than five acts can hold, more than our philosophy can encompass between heaven and earth. But at the moment he is irritated even more than usual by having to wait for the players in whom he has placed such tragic confidence. Moreover, he has just been tearing up the letters from Ophelia, who has been missing since the night before, letters which that silly little parvenue saw fit to put down on brown Holland paper so difficult to tear that Hamlet's fingers are still burning severely from the attempt. Ah, the wretchedness of such little actions! . . .

"Where can she be at this hour? Probably with her relations in the country. She'll get back all right, she knows the way. And besides she would never have understood me. When I think of it! However lovely and mortally sensitive she may have seemed, all one had to do was scratch the surface to discover a little English girl imbued since birth with the egotistical philosophy of Hobbes. 'Nothing is more agreeable about the possession of our own property than the thought that it is superior to other people's,' said Hobbes. That is the way Ophelia would have loved me, because as her 'property' I was socially and morally superior to the 'property' of her little friends. And the pretty phrases on well-being and comfort she would come out with when it was time to light the lamps! A comfortable Hamlet! Good God! Thank heaven for my Guardian Angel, if not for myself. Ah, if only on such an evening as this there might come to me, in my ivory tower, a sister, a little sister of that Helen of Narbonne who went off to Florence and won the heart of her lovely Bertrand, Count of Roussillon, although she realized his full contempt for her! . . . Ophelia, Ophelia, dear little gluey tart, come back, I implore you; I will never speak of these things again.—And besides, dear boy, Hamlet that we are, we can sometimes behave like a real bastard. Enough. Ah, here they come."

To the left, on the shores of Elsinore, he sees—and who has not heard of those marvelous sea-gull eyes?—a rowdy group that must unmistakably be the players.

The ferryman takes them into his big boat; a cur yaps at their faded finery; an urchin stops skipping stones across the water. One of the gentlemen, beautifully got-up, with the gesture of one who will stoop to anything to entertain the company, joins the ferryman at the oars, and they scud along. . . Lifted index fingers point toward the Castle, one of the ladies lets her bare arm trail in the water; and the barking, the laughter, the voices drift upward as clear as in a water color. Here are certainly the makings of a fine seventeenth-century evening.

Hamlet leaves his window, sits down at a table, and begins to leaf through two thin notebooks.

"So here we have it! My first intuition was to restage the horrible, horrible event, to exalt my filial piety, and translate everything with the full undeniability of artistic speech, to wring again from my father his last bloody cry, to warm over my plate of vengeance! And then ($\tilde{\omega}$ $\Pi\acute{o}\theta os$ $\tau o\acute{v}$ $\epsilon\acute{\iota}\nu\alpha\iota$) I began to take a liking to my little work! I forgot little by little that it concerned my murdered father, robbed of the years he had left in this precious world (poor man, poor man!). I forgot that it also concerned my mother in her rôle of prostitute (a vision which has ruined all Womanhood in my eyes and driven me to let heavenly Ophelia die of shame and deterioration), that it concerned, in a word, my right to the throne. I went merrily along arm in arm with all the fictionalized amplifications of a lovely subject. For it is certainly a lovely subject! I redid the whole thing in iambics; I threw in a good many extraneous appetizing lines; I plucked a sublime epigraph from my dear Philoctetes. Yes, I went deeper into my characters than one could ever go in life! I took all kinds of liberties with the documents! I made my genius plead for the good hero and the villainous traitor alike! And in the evening, when I had riveted the final rhyme to a principal tirade, I would go to sleep with my sweet conscience smiling at domestic chimeras, like the good literary craftsman who, by the labor of his pen, manages to support a large family! I would go to sleep without thinking of making my devotions to the two wax statuettes, and of screwing the needle in their hearts! Ah, what a hopeless ham, what a vulgar little monster am I!"

And the young insatiable prince throws himself on his knees before the portrait of his father and kisses the feet depicted on the cold canvas.

"Forgive me, forgive me, won't you, Father? You do really understand me, I know . . ."

Hamlet rises, unable to avoid that paternal eye, still winking in spite of everything below the regal faunlike brow:

"After all, everything is based on heredity. Let us be medical and naturalistic, and we will end up seeing clearly."

He returns to his manuscripts, over which he broods with his own regal faunlike eye.

"All the same, there are some charming pages here, and if the time were more propitious! Ah, why am I not a simple cleric in Paris, on Mount Ste Geneviève where that school of Neo-Alexandrians is flourishing! Or a simple little librarian at that brilliant

Valois court! Instead of inhabiting this humid castle, this den of jackals and boors where one is not even sure of one's own skin! . . ."

Two taps of a golden key on the silver knocker at the door have just sounded. Enter a footman.

"The two stars of the troupe are here, as your Highness ordered."

"Send them in."

"And Her Majesty, the Queen, wishes to know if your Highness still insists on having the play presented this very evening."

"To be blunt, why not?"

"Because, as Your Highness knows, the funeral of the Lord Chamberlain Polonius will also take place this evening, shortly."

"Well, that's a fine thing to take into account! All I can say is that some of us go on stage while others retire to the wings. And the Ideal will go on functioning to its fullest every evening just as it sees fit, my dear boy."

The footman withdraws, closing the door behind the two bowing actors.

"Come in, my friends. Sit down and have a cigarette. Which would you like, a Dubeck or a Bird's Eye? Make yourselves completely at home. And what is your name, young man?"

"William," replies the young leading man, the slashes of whose doublet are still noticeably dusty.

"And your name, young lady? (God, what a beauty! More trouble, I guess! . . .)"

"Ophelia," answers the lady with a sort of sulky smile, a smile so ambiguous that one is convulsed with uneasiness, and so wicked that the young prince feels obliged to break into laughter to relieve the situation.

"What, another Ophelia in my cup! Oh, this usurious fashion that parents have of dubbing their infants with theatrical names. Ophelia isn't a name from life! It's right off the boards! Ophelia, Cordelia, Lelia, Coppelia, Camelia! For the love of poor outcast

Hamlet, haven't you got another baptismal name (baptismal, do you hear?)"

"Yes, my Lord, my name is Kate."

"Ah, that's more like it! And how much better it suits you! Let me peck at your hand, dear Kate, to pay homage to this label."

He rises, and goes to plant a lingering kiss on that forehead so suited to one called Kate. And then he turns suddenly away, walks to the window, and hides his face in his hands.

William gestures to his companion.

"Well, they weren't joking, were they? He really is."

"How is it possible?" answer the gentle blue eyes of Kate, which turn quickly toward Hamlet as he resumes his place.

Hamlet flatteringly shrugs his shoulders.

"Well, children, let's turn the title page, and cut out the colophons. What do you bring in the way of repertory?"

"We have *The Merry Wives of Saint Denis, Doctor Faustus, The Apologue of Menenius Agrippa*, and *The King of Thule*."

"You can tell me the others day after tomorrow, when you get to them. What you offer are undoubtedly noble conceptions, though not immaculate conceptions like mine. So for the present, for this very evening, in fact, you will secretly work on the play I have in hand. And moreover you'll be royally rewarded for your pains. It is a tragedy of my own composition. There are only three principal parts. There is a king, Gonzago, and a queen, Baptista; the scene is Vienna. The queen has adulterous and conspiratorial relations with her brother-in-law Claudius. One afternoon, the king is taking his siesta, sleeping off the effects of his blossoming sins under an arbor; the queen pretends to be austerely peeling strawberries to feed him when he awakens. Enter Claudius. The two accomplices exchange a silent kiss, then they proceed to melt some lead in a spoon and pour it delicately into the king's ear."

"How horrible!" Kate bursts forth, her smile dying in a sulk.

"Isn't it? Horrible, horrible! . . . As we were saying, they pour in a little melted lead, pale liquid; and poor King Gonzago dies in convulsions . . . horrible, horrible convulsions; and in a state of mortal sin, mark you. Claudius then takes off the crown, puts it on his own head, and offers his arm to the widow. The result of it all is that, come what may, William will be Claudius, and Kate the queen, as pretty a pair of monsters as ever you hope to see."

"The fact is . . ." Kate hesitates.

"The fact is . . ." declares William, "my friend and I usually prefer to enact only sympathetic rôles."

"Sympathetic? A nice lot you are! And on what grounds do you find a character sympathetic in this base world? And what of Progress, then?"

"We are at the command of our gracious lord."

"Here is the manuscript, William, I entrust it to you. Don't go and lose it. I'm quite serious. Prepare it nicely for this evening. Now look at the speeches I have marked with my pencil of bull's-blood red. They should all be underlined, and hurled at the audience. Those that I have given the accolade of the blue pencil, on the other hand, you may suppress as too episodic, although perhaps in reality . . . well, these verses, for example:

> A heart within whose dreamy gaze
> No thought of conquest is at stake!
> Art wears me out in so many ways!
> To repeat myself is such a headache!
> > Honeymoon on high,
> > Descend from the sky.

"And this:

> O soul so brave,
> Flesh proud and upright
> Myself I covet
> To be your slave."

"How utterly charming," exclaim William and Kate, as their eyes meet.

"Indeed, yes. Ah, if the times were only tidier! . . . And this, too:

> To a Nunnery, go! For Love in our day
> Is exchanged in a perfectly meaningless way
> As simple and faithless as a simple good-day."

"That's really most extraordinary," the actor affirms.

And that unfortunate creature, Hamlet, Prince of Denmark, is exultant!

"And this delightful round:

> Once there was a pretty blouse,
> With a hey-nonny-no, with a hey-nonny-no
> With two little buttons in a row,
> With two little buttons, what do you know? . . . etc.

Et caetera, et caetera! Strange indeed are the workings of fate! . . . But be sure not to omit this—it's the victory hymn of usurper Claudius, sung to the tune of *Deceptive Presentiments!* . . . you remember, I'm sure?

> I am well prepared
> To prove that God
> Will give the nod
> To this affair!

"Well, then, everything's settled. Here is the manuscript, I entrust it to you once again, my dear William. And since the play won't begin before ten o'clock I shall come backstage a little ahead of time to see how things are going. Meanwhile I hope I shall not have to be objurgatory in respect of this little honorarium?"

The two stars pocket the money and back out of the room bowing.

William declaims under his breath to his companion:

Madness is loose on the world; how quickly it can
Strike the actor of genius and the simple tradesman;
And the guard who makes his round in the dark
    Keeps it not from Denmark.

"Poor young man!" Kate fetches an angelic sigh, "and he doesn't really look a bit dangerous. . ."

Hamlet, man of action, muses for five minutes over the tragedy which is now in good hands; then becomes excited:

"There you have it. My Lord Fengo will certainly get the point. A word to the wise is sufficient! And I will have only to act, and sign my name in blood. Act! Kill! Make him disgorge his life! Kill! . . . Yesterday I got in some practice by killing Polonius. He was spying on me, hidden behind that arras representing the Massacre of the Innocents. Ah, they are all against me! And tomorrow Laertes and the day after tomorrow old Fortinbras across the way! I must act! I must murder, or I must escape! Oh, to escape! O Liberty! Liberty! To love, to live, to dream, to be famous, far from here. Oh, dear *aurea mediocritas!* Yes, what Hamlet needs is liberty.

"I don't ask anything from anyone. I am without a friend in the world; I have not a single friend to tell my sad story, to precede me everywhere and spare me the explanations that murder me. I have no nice young girl to appreciate me. Ah, yes, what I need is a nurse! A nurse devoted to her art, offering kisses only to dying men, men *in extremis*, who would not live to boast of them afterward.

"And to think that I really exist! That I have a life of my own! Eternity-in-itself before my birth, Eternity-in-itself after my death. And to think that I spend my days like this killing time! With old age coming on, hideous old age, revered and venerated by hypocritical habit-formed young ladies. I can't kick about forever in this anonymous state! And merely to leave one's memoirs behind is not enough. O Hamlet, Hamlet! If the world knew! Women would come to lay their mournful heads on your divine heart, as once they did on the body of Adonis—with a few centuries of civilization added.—Bah! What would my biography mean to women surrounded with daily bread, with love and death? It might for a moment after dinner enacted on the stage. But how different they would feel as soon as they got back home! . . .

"Men and women jointly may well admire my scruples about existence, but they will not imitate them. Nor will they be bothered by not doing so when they sit cozily together, the man who is loved and the woman who is loved. Later on, I shall be accused of having started a school! And suppose I were to mention the name of my sacred Master, my universal Master!—But ah, how lonely I am! And the age has really nothing whatever to do with it. I have five senses which attach me to life; but this sixth sense, this sense of the Infinite!—I am still young; and as long as my health lasts, what is there to worry about? Ah, but Liberty! Liberty! Yes, I will go away, I will give up my name and live among the good common people. I will find a wife who will be mine for ever and a day, and for every day. That would certainly prove, of all my ideas, the most Hamletic. But tonight I must objectify myself, I must act. Onward, Hamlet, onward, like Nature, over the graves!"

Prince Hamlet descends from his tower and strides down a long corridor whose walls are hung with monotonous views of Jutland which he honors in passing with his heroic sputum. Then he turns at a landing where the two halberdiers on duty scarcely have time to recognize him and present arms; other halberdiers, seated on surrounding benches, are busy playing knucklebones! As he goes by, Hamlet cries out to them: *"Sustine et abstine!* Liberty! Liberty!" And whistling, he descends another strairway, and finds himself under the colonnade in front of the gatekeeper's lodge.

The gatekeeper's window is open, and a cage is hanging from one of the shutters. Even before he has looked at the cage, Hamlet throws himself at it, opens it, picks up the lukewarm canary asleep within, wrings its neck between thumb and index finger, and whistling all the more allegro, hurls it to the rear of the gate-keeper's room. He strikes—although not intentionally—the head of a little girl who sits there crocheting, taking advantage of the last unraveling of light. She stops, her eyes glazed, her hands clasped, in the presence of this hideous crime.

Hamlet flies off without looking around. Then suddenly he returns, goes to the window, and then into the room. The little girl is still there, her hands clasped. He throws himself at her feet.

"Oh, forgive me, forgive me! I didn't mean to do it! Order me to make any expiation you like. I have a heart of gold of the sort you rarely find anywhere today. You do understand me, don't you?"

"Oh, my Lord, my Lord!" the little girl stammers. "Oh, if you only knew! I understand you so well! I have loved you for so long! I understand everything! . . ."

Hamlet rises. "My God, another one!" he thinks to himself. "Is your father ill?"

"No, my Lord."

"Too bad. You would certainly know how to plaster him with poultices."

"Oh, but if it were you! I would look after you so nicely!"

"Yes, of course: I'll come by again next Monday. My cancer hasn't begun to discharge yet—I can't quite make out why not. Until Monday, dear angel."

Hamlet strides off, duly comforted. It was to get in more practice that I killed that bird, he thinks.

Unfortunate Prince! He has often been in the grip of these strange destructive impulses since his father's irregular demise.

One morning very early Hamlet had gone out hunting. Thinking about it beforehand this time had kept him awake all through the night (although it might have been better to sleep on it). Armed with pins of the finest quality, he tuned up by piercing

the scarabs Providence had set in his path, leaving them to continue on their way. He tore the wings from frivolous butterflies,
decapitated snails, sliced off the hindfeet of toads and frogs,
sprinkled an anthill with saltpeter and ignited it, gathered up a
myriad little warbling nests from the bushes, and just to give
them a taste for travel, set them adrift on the neighboring stream;
all the while slashing hundreds of flowers right and left, without
the slightest regard for their pharmaceutical powers. And then,
on with the hunt! The forest, echoing with its springtime murmurs, delighted him, much the way that a torture chamber would
have pleased him with the crackling from its ovens! And finally,
that evening, after a fruitless siesta under a clump of trees that witnessed nothing, he made his way back. And then a final spasm
compelled him to lay a further levy on the victims that had been
unable to go off and die; the levy was a pound of eyeballs. He
washed his hands in them, he oiled his joints with them. Already
twitching with pain, he made his knucklebones crack. Ah, here
he had found the DEMON OF TRUTH in delightfully proving that
Justice is but a word, that everything is allowed—and for a reason, in the name of God!—against the mute and lowly creatures
of the earth.

Approaching the Castle, Hamlet, weak with insomnia and over-
excitement, had felt the vast and painful twilight closing in to
strangle him. He crept through the park, and ran to shut himself
in his dark tower; dabbing at a blinking swarm of eyeballs, eyeballs smeared with tears that could never be dried. . . Then fully
dressed he crouched under the covers of his bed, burning with a
cold sweat, weeping out the elixir of his tears. As he thought of
killing himself or at least of slashing his face in expiation, he could
hear the quick beat of his good heart, a golden heart now forever
drowned in this pool of poor immortal and pensive eyes. But the
next morning he said: "Bah, how asinine I was! And what about
wars! And what about the slaughterhouses of the ancients, and

all that! What a pitiful country bumpkin! What a corny little corndoctor I am!"

Hamlet is thus not at all affected by the irreparable murder of the little bird; it has merely served to open the valve of his animal spirits. A good thing too: and if Hamlet has not yet sensed the fact that he is likewise not in the least affected by the sad Ophelia (not in the least a poor bird!), his Guardian Angel is certainly well aware of it.

The graveyard of Elsinore covers the side of a hill off the main road twenty minutes from the city. Hamlet passes under the triple gate of the castle's encircling fortifications, where there are five or six shops patronized by the Guards, and then finds himself in the open country, which is just like the country anywhere, the sad, flat country beyond the ramparts. . .

Workmen are returning home; a wedding party stops by the road, trying to decide what entertainment the town might offer at such an hour.

Prince Hamlet is hardly ever recognized these days. The people hesitate, but do not bow. And how could they when faced with such an insignificant little character? . . . You can judge for yourself.

Having attained a rather sudden full bloom, Hamlet is of medium height; and bears, not terribly high on his body, an elongated childish head. He has reddish brown hair which tapers to a point on a perfectly saintly forehead. It is clearly parted on the right, and tumbles thin and straight over two pretty ladylike ears. His face is beardless without looking clean-shaven; it is a mask of a rather artificial but youthful pallor. His startled and candid gray-blue eyes, while often ice-cold, are sometimes heated by insomnia. (Fortunately, however, these romantically timid eyes radiate limpid and unmuddied thought; for Hamlet, who constantly lowers his gaze as if trying to touch Reality with invisible antennae, looks more like a Camaldolese monk than a crown prince of Denmark.) He has a sensual nose. His innocent mouth is usually open; but it passes quickly from an amorous half-closed position to an equivocal rooster grin, from a pout held in place by the ball and chain of the contemporary scene to the irresistible splitting laugh of a chubby fourteen-year-old urchin. The chin, alas, could hardly be called prominent; nor the angle of the lower jaw determined except on days of deathless boredom when the jawbone is thrust forward and the eyes, by the same token, recede in the vanquished brow: the entire mask is thus drawn in, aged by twenty years. He is now thirty. Hamlet has ladylike feet. His hands are firm but somewhat twisted and shriveled. On the index finger of his left hand he wears a ring set with a green enameled Egyptian scarab. He wears nothing but black, and up and down he strides, up and down, with a gait that is slow and proper, proper and slow. . .

With a gait that is slow and proper, then, Hamlet makes his way at twilight toward the graveyard.

He passes herds of proletarians, old men, women, and children, returning from their daily labors on the capitalistic chain gang, bowed by the weight of their sordid destiny.

God, thinks Hamlet. I know it as well as the next man, and probably better. The existing social order is a scandal great enough to suffocate Nature itself! And I am nothing but a feudal parasite. But what is there to get excited about? These people were born to it; it's an old story, and it won't stop them from having their honeymoons nor their fear of death; and all is well that has no end. . . Yes, indeed. Why don't you get up one fine morning and put an end to all this? Put everything to fire and sword! Crush like bedbugs castes, religions, ideas, languages! Bring back a brotherly childhood to this Earth, which is the mother of us all, and let us be put out to graze in the tropics.

> In the gardens where pure
> Instincts endure
> Let us gather
> What will cure.

Yes, and just see if they would come along! They are too unaesthetic, too fond of being tyrants in their own little houses; it will be a long time yet before they have the courage to look Infinity in the face. Let them gape in admiration at that pedestrian philanthropist, Polonius, as he cries to them: "Go out and get rich! . . ." And to think that I had my moment of apostolic folly, like Sakyamuni, who was also the son of a king. Ho, ho, I with my unique little existence (which will be shared by a unique little woman); and to think of attaching that bell to my throat! And to hear in its tinkle the wild sonorous notes within my head! Let us not be more proletarian than the proletarians. Let us not permit Human Justice to be more just than Nature. Yes, my brothers, my friends, the historic come-what-may or the apocalyptic purgative, good old Progress or back to Nature. . . And in the meantime, good appetite and enjoy yourselves: tomorrow is Sunday.

The path to the graveyard is steep. Scowling, Hamlet crumples a few poppies between his fingers. He has arrived too late; the service for Polonius is over; the last official silhouettes can be seen departing. Hamlet crouches behind a hedge to let them pass. Someone gives an arm to Laertes, the son of the deceased, who is a sad sight to contemplate. A voice, as of one who has stood all he can, exclaims: "When there's a lunatic loose in your house, the least you can do is lock him up."

As he rises, Hamlet notices that he has just gravely damaged an anthill. "So much for that," he says to himself. "And just to be sure that I put chance under obligation to me. . ." And he finishes off the said anthill with a few twists of his heel.

The mourners have gone. Hamlet finds himself alone with two gravediggers. He approaches one of them who is arranging the wreaths on Polonius' tomb.

"We won't have his bust until next month," volunteers the gravedigger whom no one has asked.

"What did he die of? Do they know?"

"Of a stroke. He had led quite a merry life."

Then and there, Hamlet, whose conscience, despite his soul's extreme cultivation, had not yet taken in the fact, realizes that he has most assuredly killed a man, suppressed a life, a life to which one can bear witness. The aforementioned Polonius . . . who from his squinting eye could have looked out on forty years more of life. (Polonius, who at the drop of a hat, would make you feel his iron muscles.) And lo, Hamlet, with one casual but fatal thrust, has scratched out those forty years just as one would make an erasure on some extravagant blueprint. And what can all these trifling little conflicts of phenomena mean in the next world?

Hamlet plants himself in front of the gravedigger who gazes out at him, waiting to be complimented on the arrangement of the wreaths; Hamlet looks down his nose at him and then barks in his face: "Words, words, words! Do you hear me? Words, words, words!"

And then he walks over to the other gravedigger without hearing the first one call after him, "On your way, you loafer!"

"And what are you doing, my good man?"

"As Your Lordship can see, I am sprucing up the old tombs. Ah, it's been a good long time since any of the old birds have moved in here. Our little cemetery has never increased in size, although the late king, through his bounteous favors, redoubled the population of his fine city."

The gravedigger, who is slightly tipsy, tries to support himself on his spade.

"Well, what do you know, doubled the population? . . ."

"One can see that Your Lordship is not of these parts. The late king (who incidentally also died of a stroke) was quite a womanizer, and being a handsome man with a heart of gold, wherever he left offspring, he also left the stamp of his likeness in the ladies' hearts and on the coins in their purses."

"But Prince Hamlet surely is the son of the king's wife, Gerutha, is he not?"

"Far from it! Your Lordship has probably heard of the late fool, the incomparable Yorick."

"Yes, indeed."

"Well, he and Prince Hamlet had the same mother."

Hamlet the brother of a court fool; then he isn't of such pure lineage as he had thought! . . .

"And that mother, who was she?"

"Well, the mother was the most hellishly beautiful gypsy any-one, by your leave, has ever seen. With her son Yorick, she came here telling fortunes. She was retained by the Castle, and died a year later, giving birth to the noble Hamlet; when I say giving birth—she died of the Caesarean that had to be performed."

"Ah, that fellow Hamlet was not so easily drawn into this low world then! . . ."

"Exactly. She was buried there where Your Lordship can see we've been digging lately. An order came not long ago from the Queen to exhume her remains and burn them, although the gypsy was a Christian like you and me, the proof being that the day we carried out the order we got royally soused. And now it's poor Yorick's turn; his bones are right there where your Lordship can grind them under foot."

"I'll do no such thing."

"And now I must get his tomb ready to receive Polonius' noble daughter, Ophelia. They've found her body, and will be bringing it here in an hour. Well, I suppose we all must die sooner or later."

"Ah, Ophelia . . . they have found that young lady, have they? . . ."

"Near the dam, Sir. Her brother Laertes came to tell us this morning. He was a pitiful sight, the poor young man. Everybody likes him so much. He takes a great interest in the living condi-tions of the workers, you know. And, believe me, I could tell you about some strange things that go on."

"And I suppose they're quite sure now that Prince Hamlet has gone mad? (Oh, my God, my God, by the dam . . .)"

"Yes, this is the end. As I have always said, we are ripe for an-
nexation. Prince Fortinbras of Norway will see to it any day
now. I've already invested my little pickings in Norwegian
stocks. But all of that won't stop me from getting good and drunk
tomorrow."

"Right you are. Carry on."

Hamlet puts a crown in the man's hand, and picks up Yorick's
skull. With a slow and proper gait, he wanders off among the
cypresses and mausoleums, so overwhelmed by shady destinies
that he can't make out how he can with any decency resume his
rôle.

Hamlet stops; he holds Yorick's skull tight against his ear, and
listens, lost in thought. . .

"Alas, poor Yorick! Just as one thinks he hears within a single
shell the full roar of the Ocean, so I seem to hear now the whole
endless symphony of the universal soul, of which this sounding
box was an echoing crossroad.

"What a sound idea that is! To have human beings like me who
would not ask themselves questions but would find in the vague
immortal rumor of the skull all they need know of death, all they
need know of religion! Alas, poor Yorick! The little worms have
tasted Yorick's intellect. He was a fellow of fairly infinite jest,
my brother (for we had, after all, the same mother for nine
months of our lives, if that can be said to entitle us to any special
status). He was someone. How stuck up he was with his twisted
and cunning little ego! And where has all that got him? No one
will ever know. There's nothing now, not even the wraith of the
sleepwalker; common sense leaves no traces. Once there was a
tongue in this head and it would burr: *Good night, ladies; good
night, sweet ladies! good night, good night!* It would sing, too;
it would often sing smutty songs. Yorick looked into the future!
(Hamlet swings the skull forward.) And into the past. (He brings
it back.) He spoke, he blushed, he YAWNED! Horrible, horrible.

I may still have twenty or thirty years to live, and then I'll go like the others. Like the others? Oh, like all things, terrible! Not to be? Ah, I'd like to start out tomorrow and look everywhere on earth for the most adamantine embalming processes. They also existed, the little people of History, learning to read, doing their nails, lighting their dirty lamps every evening, amorous, greedy, vain, delighting in compliments, handshakes and kisses, eating up the village gossip, saying: "What will the weather be tomorrow? Now winter is coming . . . We have had no plums this year." Ah, all is well that has no end. Forgive the Earth, O Silence! The little fool isn't any too sure what she's doing; and on the day Conscience pays its staggering bill to the Ideal, it will be set down with sad ditto marks in the column of miniature evolutions of the Unique Evolution, in the column of negligible quantities. But these are words, words, words! That will be my motto until someone has proved to me that our speech has some connection with a transcendent reality. As for me, with my genius, I might be what is commonly called a Messiah; and yet I have been too much Nature's spoiled darling for that. I understand everything, I worship everything, and I want to fertilize everything. That is why, as I have expressed it in this limping distich carved above my bed:

> My rare faculty of assimilation
> Goes counter to the course of my vocation.

Ah, how masterly is my boredom! . . . But what am I waiting for? Death! Death! Ah, have I time to think about death, such a gifted being as I? And as for dying, really! There will be time to talk about that later. Dying! One dies of course without noticing it just as one goes to sleep at night. One cannot follow the fading of one's last clear thought in sleep, in fainting, or in death. True. But not to be, not to be anywhere, not to be anyone! Not to be able to sit down some afternoon just to press the ancient sadness of a musical chord against one's human heart! My father is dead;

I am the prolongation of a body that no longer exists. He is over there stretched out on his back with his hands clasped in front of him. And what can I do but lie down when my turn comes? And people will not laugh when they look at me, properly stretched out, my hands clasped in front of me! And they will wonder: Can this be the spoiled young Hamlet, who was once so bitter and gay? There he is as serious as everyone else; and he did not rebel against the crying injustice of being there, but accepted it with such quiet dignity?"

With his two hands Hamlet clasps the skull of his skeleton to be, and tries to force a shiver through all his bones.

"Come, come! Let's be serious now! I must find words, words, words! But what is it that I lack, if all this leaves me cold. Let me see. When I am hungry, I have an intense vision of comestibles; when I am thirsty I have a clear sense of liquids; when I feel too celibate at heart, I have a heart-rending sense of lovely eyes and graceful epidermis. Then if the idea of death remains so remote to me, it must be because I am overflowing with life, because life has me in its grip and wants something from me. So, Life, let the two of us have it out!"

"Hey, you over there!" the second gravedigger calls out, "here is Ophelia's funeral procession coming up."

Pensive Hamlet's first impulse is to ape perfectly a clown awakened by a huge drumstick in his back; but he manages to restrain himself. Then he slips behind a trefoiled balustrade and gets ready to keep an eye on things.

The melancholy procession is drawing to a close—once and for all! In the jolting of the ascent, some white roses have fallen from the black velvet covering the coffin—have fallen, alas, once and for all!

"She's not really very heavy," Hamlet thinks with interest. "But I was forgetting; she must be swollen with water like a goatskin bag. Dirty little thing, fished up by the dam! After she'd soaked herself so aimlessly in my library, how else could she end?

Oh, my God! Now I can appreciate those big blue eyes of hers! Poor young lady! So thin and heroic! So chaste and inviolate! This is the end, the end. In the none-too-distant future that lady-killer Fortinbras would have added her to his harem. And since I had made her what she was, I know that she would have died of shame! She would have expired, leaving only a scandalous Fair Helen's reputation behind her. But now, thanks to me . . ."

For a moment Hamlet is lost in watching the monks officiate around the grave; they lose no time, these monks, for tomorrow is Sunday, and they will have their hands full. A young lady is as quickly buried as she is married. Who can find time to argue with that? Art is so long and life, so short! And for his humble part, Hamlet can't help feeling his nerves contract with a tingling of remorse.

"All the same! How could someone as good-hearted, as golden-hearted as I, have done such a thing! Fie, Hamlet, fie! . . . Poor Ophelia, poor dear; she was my childhood sweetheart. And I loved her! That's obvious, self-evident! I couldn't ask anything better than to be regenerated by her smile. But Art is so great and life is so short! And nothing is feasible. I was damned in advance by my mother and my brother, by everything. (Yes, there's something in that.) And as a result, the pain I could not avoid causing her kept her so miserably thin that the engagement ring which I had in better days slipped on her finger was constantly falling off, a proof from heaven that. . . And besides, she looked much too perishable! And since the girls here are already wearing low-necked evening dresses at the age of sixteen, her shoulders had lost the charm of a virginity to be ravaged. The devil take me if I can recall when I saw those shoulders for the first time! Now everybody knows that the virginity of the shoulders is everything to me; it's something on which I never compromise. But she ended up looking just like the others, despite her uplifted heavenly gaze. So I was robbed. There was nothing left for me to do after that but observe her little feminine gestures.

What eyes, I used to think, can I ever believe in now? I should have put out those eyes; I should have washed my hands with them. And then, too, that infernal voice of hers which always awaited me at our appointments and made my head spin with its talk of *kisses!* No! Positively! No—words, words, words! It would have driven me mad. I must get a grip on myself.

"Go on, go on, droning your *Holy, holy, holy, Lord God Almighty!* The divine personality, what an idea! That's what you really call creating personalities. Her heaven is still my memory. Because she did have what I shall always ask of the fiancée worthy of my genius, and that was a mouth which was ingenuously welcoming, but which was guarded by two large knowing eyes, or rather—like that actress Kate's, I must admit—two delicately roving credulous blue eyes guarded by a mouth whose bitter little corner fold indicated that it is eternally on the defensive. And her profile—and the profile is, after all, the only standard by which to measure a woman's beauty—did not recall that of any animal, whether bulldog or gazelle. And even in our most intimate moments, I never detected any trace of the bitch. In brief, she was a saint in a simple petticoat. It would have been a shame for her to grow old. And to become the mistress of Fortinbras! Ah, Ophelia, why weren't you born to be my life-companion, why did you have to be too famous for that! I helped her to wither and fate did the rest.

> Ophelia, Ophelia,
> Your body adrift
> Stirs like a whip
> My old folly . . ."

The ceremony is drawing to its close—once and for all. One can hear the soft chunks of earth tolling on the coffin, tolling on the coffin, alas, once and for all! . . .

"Well, as I was saying, she had an angelic torso. But what can

I do about all that now? Listen, God, I will give ten years of my life to bring her back to life. No answer. Going, going, gone! Either there is no God, or else I haven't got ten years left to give. The first hypothesis seems to me the more likely of the two, and for a very good reason."

Hamlet, being a man of action, naturally doesn't leave his hiding place until he is sure that the brutal Laertes has filed out with the rest of the honorable company.

"Brother Yorick, I am taking your skull home with me. I'll give it a place of honor among my sacred souvenirs, between one of Ophelia's gloves and my first tooth. Ah, how I must work this winter with all this new material! I have an infinite supply of the infinite."

Night is falling, and the time for action has come! Hamlet takes the road back to the castle, relatively unmoved by the everyday aspect of night on the highway. He climbs to his tower to deposit the skull, that powerful knick-knack. He leans out the window for a moment to watch the lovely full moon reflected in gold on the calm sea where it unwinds a broken column of black velvet and liquid gold, aimless but magical.

Like this moonlight on the melancholy water . . . so the blessed Ophelia drifted through the night to her damnation.

"And yet I can't kill myself, I can't deprive myself of life! Ophelia, Ophelia! Forgive me! Don't cry like that!"

Hamlet goes back into his room and gropes around feverishly in the darkness.

"I cannot bear the sight of a young lady's tears. To make a young lady cry, it seems to me, is more irreparable than to marry her. Because tears belong to children; young ladies shed tears only when they feel a grief so deep that all their years of social and rational hardening break through and are drowned in a spring that gushes forth from childhood, from the primitive creature incapable of evil. Farewell, lovely eyes of Ophelia, eyes that were not violated because they could not be tamed! Night has come, and the time for action. Kisses and theories must wait until to-morrow."

Hamlet goes down to see how his play is coming on.

A corridor, which is usually filled with extra supplies of re-freshments for the court balls, has been divided into dressing rooms, and serves as wings for the stage.

Without giving it much thought, Hamlet pushes one of the dressing-room doors gently, and goes in. He stops on the thresh-old. There before his eyes, among the unpacked trunks, weeping like a Magdalen, hiccoughing with the final sobs of a crying spell, the actress Kate is lying on the floor. She has put on a gown of red and gold lamé with a long train but not yet a bodice. With arms and shoulders bare, her lovely breasts showing through a delicately pleated shirtwaist, she lies there, poor creature, in a state suggesting that she might welcome consolation.

Hamlet closes the door deftly and dextrously behind him, and prepares to embark on this new adventure.

"Well, Kate, what's all this? What's wrong with you?"

The lovely Kate is not the least bit disturbed by the presence of His Royal Highness. She lies prostrated a few minutes longer in the superiority of her tears and of her refound childhood. Then, since one must always end by doing something, she stands up; and without concerning herself further with His Highness except to turn her back on him, she resumes the organization of her disordered person as a queen for the night, and with her re-maining tears rages against the knots in her laces.

Ah, how bounteous is her beauty, in spite of everything! There is no doubt about it, if she speaks to him, if she speaks to him and runs along the Hamletic coast without getting her feet wet, Hamlet is lost! Lost and won!

"Come now, it can't be as bad as all that. What's the matter, Kate, my love?"

And he takes her gently by the waist.

"Tell me, tell me all."

The lovely Kate gives him an immortal look, and then lets herself go. She hides her face on the bosom of the chaste prince, and bursts into tears again, shedding all her tears on the black velvet doublet which only last month had absorbed Ophelia's quota.

Hamlet feels obliged to sow her neck with all sorts of kisses, calming or not so calming, while he smooths the braids of her hair.

Only Hamlet's pen could picture Kate's beauty. Kate is one of those apparitions that stop you dead in the street. You don't think of turning to follow. (What would be the use, you say to yourself, since her life must certainly be arranged already?) One of those women in a drawing room at whom you gaze indifferently and distantly rather than ardently, madly, and tenderly. (How accustomed she must be to seeing bewildered heads turn toward her, you think; why give oneself the trouble of swelling the mob?) Then you learn that she lives somewhere or other, married or single, just like anyone else. And you are astonished to discover that she is not the famous So-and-So, who, although she is only twenty-five and looks like a little beast that has always slept comfortably the night before, has been the center of international complications.

And Kate, who has been around quite a bit in her day, has been around in nothing less than epic fashion! And oh, how miserably! One-night stands, shaded lights, banging doors, filthy go-betweens. O poverty, O bargains! She has been around in her day, and yet there she is, looking right at you. And her puckered lips form a delicate bellflower that has just opened this morning, and her large mysterious eyes seem to burst out with "Yes? . . . Ah? . . ." and what modesty there is in the soft knot of hair on that slender neck! . . . But enough of this! She is merely one of the opposite sex, a slave who knows not what she does. . .

She hardly knows what she does, and Hamlet hardly knows what to do except to let his pouting, adolescent lips wander in a pitying caress over the delicately rinsed flesh of her sorrowing shoulders, and to show himself a human being, a simple human being.

But no! Such simple solutions lie a long way off. We must make a clean sweep of everything this very evening!

"Now, dearest Kate, you who had never laid eyes on me before yesterday but find my kisses so natural this evening, you must explain these tears. You must tell me what's wrong."

"Oh, no, never!"

"Is it as ugly as all that? Come now, let me . . ."

And while the rest of the sentence trails off over the shoulders he plies with kisses, she looks straight at him, lowers her eyes, stretches out her arms, and says rather vexedly but with an air of complete and utter boredom:

"Well, then! I may be nothing but a poor wretch, but my soul is definitely superior, and don't forget it for a minute. God knows what sublime heroines I have enacted in my day. But when I read my scenes of childhood and first betrothal in that peculiar play of yours, oh! Yes, you have it all down, our poor pitiful pitiless destiny! Oh, how unique and misunderstood you must be! And not mad either, as these tooth-picking, spur-clanking fools would have it. And how you must have made others suffer, too! Well, there it is, it is all quite simple . . . But no, no!"

"Go on, go on, Ophelia."

"Well, then. As I was dressing, I was saying over to myself the monologue in the church, and suddenly my heart broke again and gave way to tears, and I let myself sink to the floor. If you only knew the vastness of my heart! Ah, I've had enough of this cynical and empty existence! I will leave everything tomorrow, I will go back to Calais and enter a convent and devote my life to the poor wounded veterans of the Hundred Years War."

Hamlet, despite his natural reserve, can hardly contain his artistic satisfaction. This is his poetic baptism, and this young actress brings him the baptismal package, all nicely done up, from the most famous theatre in London. And now Hamlet belabors poor Kate for details, and makes her go over it all word for word; he puts his whole cosmic heart into admiring himself in these knowing eyes which his genius has just enlarged with glory.

"So you think the reception over the footlights of the theatrical capitals would be terrific? And that people would pause in the streets to marvel at my mournful gait? And that some of them would kill themselves when faced with the enigma of my life? O Kate, if you only knew! This tragedy is nothing; it was conceived and executed during the most repulsive domestic difficulties. But here in my brain I have other poems and plays, extraordinary magic and metaphysic that can either strike like thunder or give slow death! Ah, come Kate, I'll give up everything, too, and we'll love each other. We'll set out this evening in this lovely lucid moonlight! I'll read you everything I've written! Come, let's go live in Paris."

Kate goes on weeping quietly.

"No, no Hamlet. That isn't for me. I must withdraw from the world, enter a nunnery and care for the wounded veterans of the utterly disastrous Hundred Years War, and pray for you."

A light knock at the door.

"Come, Kate, dry those interesting eyes of yours. Hook up your dress. I will be back before the end of the play. I love you, love you! And you will tell me more about this great big wonderful thing. . . Come in!"

It is the director; Hamlet murmurs to him in passing: "Be sure to keep my secret now! This play is not by me. You are just giving the first piece in your repertory. Go to it!"

"Damn it all," Hamlet continues audibly as he climbs the stairs back to his room, "I don't care any more about this play and its moral lesson than I do about Kate's first lover! . . . The die is cast! I have the whole thing solved. Solutions always come from where one least expects them. For me, there is life and life's surrounding territory, with a great deal of glorious pessimism thrown in."

Hamlet dresses fully, and chooses some etchings which he packs with manuscripts, gold and jewelry into two chests. He selects a few pistols. Then he lights a stove, and places a copper engraving plate on top of it. On the copper plate he lays the two statuettes with their hearts childishly pierced by a needle, and the two statues soon begin to flow toward each other, uniting tenderly in a most repulsive pool.

"I don't give a damn about my throne either. It's too idiotic. Fortinbras of Norway would advise me to look at it that way. Well and good. The dead are dead. I'm off to see the world. And Paris! I am sure she acts like an angel, a terrific little angel. What a hit we'll be with our fantastic stage names!"

Hamlet tries to think of a fantastic stage name; but no: in his mind, he is already galloping with her through space. And tomorrow on Sunday when the little girls are at mass and vespers as usual, he and Kate will be far, pathetically far, from the ramparts of Elsinore!

Hamlet rings for his groom to make some final arrangements; and while waiting, amuses himself by sending a few jets of saliva at the canvases hung on the walls of his room, those views of Jutland that have weighed on his undernourished, unproductive youth.

King Fengo and Queen Gerutha drag through the hall their weary, affable smiles and are installed in their stalls. The audience sits down with the indecisive rustling of a field of golden grain leaning to see which way the wind is blowing. The pages walk back toward the doors. The curtain parts.

In a dark corner of the gallery, Hamlet, to whom nobody ever pays the slightest attention, is seated on a cushion and observes the hall and the stage through the arches of the balustrade.

The hackneyed phrase, "the agitated throng," forms on his lips. . . Come, Hamlet, let all this leave you impervious and cold. The audience is a cipher, court etiquette forbids applause, and people will model their faces on those of the royal pair. After the second act, they are sure to lose their composure and their impartiality.

The play begins. Hamlet knows it by heart. He is wholly absorbed by the scenic effects, notes in advance the force of the words on a live audience, and ruminates on possible alterations. Kate enters at last, and electrifies the play.

"By Jove, I was nothing but a schoolboy! The test of the footlights, that's what I needed! Oh, I haven't given up half what I have in my guts. And Kate! How perfectly bewitching she is, with that Roman bob! She doesn't seem to know where she is being led: one minute her eyes know everything, everything there is to know, by heaven, and the next minute they know nothing, absolutely nothing. Truly, her whole being is designed to accomplish things people will be discussing a thousand years from now. We understand one another so beautifully. What a hit we'll be! She has the same uplifted look that Ophelia had, but it gives her a real lift. (I ought to make a note of that one!) I want to love her like life. . . How well she read those lines:

> Oh, come back, my beloved, come
> Back to weep in my long hair;
> Bracelets of promises I'll make for you there,
> You'd like them would you? Here, take some! . . .

"Oh, I'm coming, you can bet I'm coming! And I who thought I knew all about Women. Women and Freedom! And all I did was soil them with *a priori* banalities. Vulgar pedant! Corny chiropodist that I am! . . . And the two criminals down there, they are really taking in the show, those two. They haven't yet begun to suspect the origin of this horrible, horrible drama. I may have allowed myself too many little fantastical excrescences, and some of them remain in spite of my cuts. But let's wait for the scene in the garden. . . What, Laertes isn't here?"

The audience rises for the intermission. After the pages have lifted up their trains, the king and queen sweep about the room, promenading their affable, weary smiles.

Trays of sliced herring are passed around, and aurochs' horns foaming with mead.

When in scene two of the next act the curtain opens on King Gonzago being fanned to sleep by his wife in front of the grape arbor, Fengo the Rabbit-Heart understands; and without waiting for the entrance of Claudius, crumples up in a faint. The queen stands up straight, very much Paul Delaroche. The courtiers press forward with a whole repertory of looks and whispers. With a blow of his halberd, Polonius' successor, happy to have the opportunity to inaugurate his functions as lord chamberlain, rings down the curtain on the horrible, horrible play.

Hamlet leaps to his feet, stammering:

"Music, music! So it's true! And I still only half believed it! . . . Well, this has been punishment enough for them in my opinion. As for me, I'm taking off! If I stayed around one day more, they would poison me like a rat, a filthy rat."

He rushes down the service stairs, which resound with bells and buzzers. The wings of the stage are deserted. The first thing Hamlet does is pick up the manuscript of his play, with the page open at the point of interruption.

Kate is there waiting for him.

"It was just a fainting spell. I'll tell you all about it later. But let me embrace you. Your acting was divine. Now we haven't a minute to lose . . . like two rats!"

He helps her out of her brocade. She had the practical idea of wearing her own frock underneath. Hamlet wraps her in a mantle and caps her with a toque.

"Quick. Follow me."

They cross the park, and Hamlet's gay whistle scatters the sleeping birds. They go out through a little gate. A groom is there, holding two horses by their bridles.

As soon as they get into the saddles between the precious boxes, they are off—at a trot, naturally. (But no, it's impossible! It has all happened much too quickly!)

They by-pass the main gate of Elsinore, and cut across the fields to reach the highway, the highway still without the moon, the moon which will soon be doing its noble best on plain after plain. . .

It is the same road along which Hamlet was walking a few hours before when he met the day-laboring proletarians.

A lovely evening; the earth seems heated by some heavenly furnace. And the moon, not without success, is playing the northern capitals.

"Kate, did you have supper before the performance?"

"No, I didn't really have the heart to eat under the circumstances."

"I haven't had a bite since noon. In an hour, we'll come to a hunting lodge where we can have something. The caretaker is my foster father. He has a picture of me as a baby."

Hamlet notices that they are just passing the graveyard.

(The Graveyard . . .)

And there, responding to heaven knows what mysterious urge, he gets down from his horse and ties it to an unimportant melancholy tree.

"Wait one minute, will you, Kate? I want to glance at the tomb of my poor murdered father! I'll tell you all about it later. I'll be back in a moment—I just want to pick a flower, a simple paper flower, that we can use as a bookmark when we interrupt the reading of our little drama to exchange kisses."

He wanders off among the shadows cast by the cypresses on the stones, and goes straight to the tomb of Ophelia, who is by now mysterious and legendary. There, with his arms crossed, he pauses.

"Well, really and truly, now . . .

> Those who are dead
> Are quite discreet;

> They go to bed
> Right in the street."

"Who goes there? Is that you, cursed Hamlet? What are you doing here?"

"It's you, my dear Laertes. By what happy chance? . . ."

"Yes, it is; and if you weren't a poor demented creature who is irresponsible according to the newest scientific discoveries, you would pay with your head right now for the death of my honorable father, and that accomplished young lady, my sister. There, on their tombs!"

"O Laertes, it's all one to me. But you can be sure that I will take your point of view into consideration. . ."

"Good Heavens, what an absence of moral sense!"

"Then you believe it really happened?"

"Away from here, you lunatic, or I will forget myself! When a man goes mad, it's because he began by acting like it."

"And your sister!"

"Oh."

At this moment one can hear through the spectrally clear night the superhumanly desolate sound of a farmer's watchdog baying at the moon; and the heart of this good Laertes, who—too bad that I think of it so late—should properly have been the hero of this tale, breaks, breaks with the inexplicable anonymity of his thirty years! This is absolutely too much to take! And seizing Hamlet's throat with one hand, with the other he plants a somewhat realistic dagger in his heart.

Our hero sinks to his knees on the grass. He gulps up blood like an animal doomed to die. He attempts to speak . . . and manages somehow to utter:

"Ah, ah, *Qualis* . . . *artifex* . . . *pereo!*"

And then he renders unto everlasting nature his Hamletic soul.

Laertes, humanity's idiot, leans down, kisses the poor dead man on the forehead and shakes his hand. Then he stumbles off through the dark and leaps over the wall. He will probably become a monk and never return.

Silence and moon . . . Graveyard and nature . . .

"Hamlet! Hamlet!" Soon Kate's quavering voice calls out: "Hamlet! . . ."

The moon bathes everything in a polar silence.

Kate decides to come and see for herself.

And she does. She runs her hand over the corpse livid with moonlight and death.

"Good Heaven, he has stabbed himself."

She leans over the tomb, and reads:

OPHELIA

DAUGHTER OF LORD POLONIUS AND LADY ANNE

DIED AT EIGHTEEN YEARS OF AGE

And at the bottom, today's date.

"She was the one he loved! Then why did he carry me off so lovingly? Poor hero . . . What on earth shall I do?"

She leans down, kisses him, calls to him.

"Hamlet, *my little Hamlet!*"

But death is death, as everybody has known since life began.

"I will go back to the castle with the horses, I will find the groom who witnessed our departure, and I will tell everything."

She sets off at the same trot, turning her back on the full moon, which was to do so well by one plain after another on its way toward Paris and the brilliant Valois, who are holding plenary court.

So when they found out about everything, the reprehensible trickery of the play, the abduction, etc., they went to look for the corpse. And they carried the most exquisite torches. And why should they not be exquisite on such an historic evening?

Now Kate was, of course, William's mistress.

"Aha!" that fellow exclaimed, "you were trying to run out on Baby, eh?"

(Baby is short for Billy, the diminutive of William.)

And Kate received a good sound drubbing which was not her first and which was not to be her last, more is the pity! And yet Kate was so lovely that in the Golden Age of Greece men would have built altars to do her honor.

And so order was restored.

One Hamlet less does not mean the end of the human race. Of that you may be sure.

THE MIRACLE OF THE ROSES

The other bed of sensitive plants behaved rather differently, for the cotyledons drooped in the morning until eleven thirty, then rose; but after twelve ten, they fell again. And the great ascensional movement of the evening did not begin until one twenty-two.

—Darwin

Never, never, never, was that little watering place aware of anything—the little watering place with its vulgar municipal council elected by avaricious mountaineers whose only lightness lay in their light-opera costume.

Ah, why isn't everything light opera! . . . Why doesn't everything revolve to the tune of that English waltz "Myosotis," which they played so often that year at the Casino, while I sat dejected in a corner, as you can well imagine—a waltz so properly melancholy, evoking so irrevocably the last, last lovely days! . . . (If I could only, with a word, make you drunk with the spirit of that waltz before allowing you to enter my little tale.)

O gloves never touched by cleaning fluid! O brilliant and melancholy comings and goings of those lives! O forgivable appearances of happiness! O beauties growing old in black lace by the fireside, without ever understanding the behavior of the strong lively sons to whom they had given birth with such modest melancholy! . . .

Little town, little town of my heart.

Now invalids no longer walk round and round the Springs, holding their carefully graduated glasses. Now baths are the thing —water at 25 degrees centigrade—then a stroll and a nap; baths for neurotics, and especially for women and for the womanly who are in such bad shape.

You see them wandering about, these good neurotics, dragging feet that will never again waltz to the delicate formal air of "Myosotis," or pushed about on the frayed leather of their wheelchairs.

You see them suddenly leave their seats during concerts at the Casino, emitting those peculiar sounds of involuntary swallowing; you see them whirl around in the course of their walks, bringing their hands to their necks as if some joker had just slashed them with a razor. You meet them in the woods, their disturbed faces twitching, strewing bits of torn letters in the antediluvian ravines. These are the neurotics, children of too brilliant a century; you find them everywhere.

Here, as elsewhere, the kindly sun, lover of snakes, cemeteries, and waxdolls, also attracts a few consumptives, slow of step but dear to the dilettante.

In better days they used to gamble at the Casino. (O brilliant and irresponsible days mourned by this foolish heart!) Since the gambling has stopped—O shade of Prince Canino, your faithful Leporello still at your side, what inglorious gravedigger tends you now?—the rooms are sad indeed, the rooms with their guards in brass-buttoned blue uniforms are quite deserted. But in the reading room, still well stocked with newspapers, there is always one or the other of the neurotics to drive you out: the noise of their involuntary swallowing makes the copy of the *Temps* fall from your hands. The old gaming room has nothing to offer but Dutch tops and Jockey billiards, showcases filled with prizes for childish lotteries, and tables in the corners for chess and checkers. Another room acts as storage space for the grand piano of yesteryear— O incurably romantic ballades of Chopin, you have put another generation to rest, while the girl who plays you this morning is in *love*, and believes that love was unknown in the world before her, before the arrival of her distinguished and matchless heart: she laments, O Ballades, your inglorious exile! Now no one lifts this piano's faded chintz cover; but the breezes of lovely evenings try out strange harmonica arpeggios on the crystal stalactites of a chandelier that once lit up so many plump shoulders dancing to the naughty tunes of Offenbach.

Ah, from the terrace of the naughty Casino of old one looks

out on a thick grassy tennis court. On this healthy expanse all the truly modern, muscled makers of history, fresh from their showers, give vent to their animal spirits, their bare arms and proud bodies ready to take charge of the educated and free young ladies, who go elegantly limping about in low-heeled shoes, holding up their heads to fresh air and to Man . . . (Instead of cultivating their immortal souls and meditating on death and illness, as good Christians should.)

Beyond this greensward of modern youth lie the slopes of the first hills and the Greek chapel with gilded cupolas, to whose vaults are relegated the royal remains of the princes of Stourdza.

And farther on, the Villa X. in which sulks a fallen Catholic queen, rather illiterate to tell the truth, whose guest book these days is almost bare of names, but who still thinks of herself as the great drawing-card of the district.

And then more hills, touched-up color plates of romantic towers and picture-postcard cottages.

And above this ridiculous little town and its encircling hills stretch the infinite heavens, which are lost to these delicate ladies: they never step out, in fact, without putting a frivolous umbrella between themselves and God.

The Entertainment Committee does a fine job: Venetian evenings, balloon ascensions (the balloonist is always called Karl Securius), merry-go-rounds, séances of spiritualism and anti-spiritualism—all to the accompaniment of a valiant little band that nothing in the world could prevent from trooping to the Springs at half past seven every morning to play its overture for the day. Then in the afternoon under the acacias of the Promenade—O solos of the little harpist who dresses in black, blanches her face with powder, and lifts her eyes to the roof of the bandstand, hoping to be snatched away by some exotic invalid whose soul trembles like her harp strings! Then in the evening under the indispensable electric light—O March from *Aïda* on the cornet, ascending to the indubitable and fantastic stars! . . .

There you have it, the little luxurious spa. There it is like an elegant hive tucked away in a valley. All these wandering couples are rich with a past spent heaven knows where; and no proletarians in sight—Oh, would that all European capitals were nice little watering places!—the only underlings on view are those that luxury offers, grooms, coachmen, cooks in white on the stoops in the evening, donkey drovers, and drivers of the cows that provide milk for the consumptives. And every language and every human type of the civilized world.

At twilight when the band is playing and one yawns a bit, lifting one's eyes to this eternal circle of trim green hills and to the people strolling round and round with pale, intense smiles, one has indeed the maddening sensation of being in a luxurious prison, with its green exercise ground, and that the prisoners are invalids suffering from a romantic past, banished here far from the serious capitals where Progress continues on its merry way.

We used to take supper on the terrace. Not far away was the table of Princess T., a big, badly built, overrated brunette who thought herself a wit (what a mistake!) surrounded by her little group who shared her opinion (another mistake!) . . . I would sit and watch the fountain leap diabolically toward Venus as it rose on the horizon. Waking echoes from the valley, rockets also climbed, rockets like other fountains or perhaps more like the stars, stars as indubitable and fantastic to both fountain and rocket as to the March from *Aïda* fulminating nostalgically from that thinking reed, the cornet. How ineffable those evenings were! You who were there and who had not yet drawn, as a lightning rod draws lightning, your unknown fiancée, look no more, for the one you would find today would surely be another, a substitute, a poor substitute.

O little town, you once were my only love, but now no longer. Since she—She—has died, I rarely return, I have hardly anything more to do with you; not because of sentimentality, although sentimentality is not all that frivolous people take it to be, but because of an indefinable something that has no name in any language, something like the voice of the blood.

—— II ——

It was Corpus Christi Day.

Since early morning the old bells had been tolling.

> O bells, bells, bells, my bells that ring,
> What divine reproaches you must bring . . .

But too much in contrast with the divine bells were certain mean-spirited rivalries. There was, of course, to be a procession, and the main square was its most important stop, and on this square every year the two hotels, the Hôtel d'Angleterre and the Hôtel de France renewed the painful rivalries of Waterloo and the Grand-Prix, in the decoration of their altarpieces.

Public opinion (*vox populi, vox Dei*) for a second time had given the palm to the Hôtel d'Angleterre.

And understandably so, for besides the classical arrangement on the copper-rodded carpeting of four holy pictures with flower stands and candelabra ablaze in the June sunlight, this lair of Albion's sons exhibited, in a confusion of palm fans at the top of the steps, a Saint Theresa, patron saint of the town, whose hysterical rococo polychrome corrupted the eye. The Hôtel de France, on the other hand, hadn't been able to think of anything better to do than intensify its floral orgy of the preceding year.

On the third side of the square, the palace of the Duchess H. interposed, for the maintenance of good form and the edification of the masses, the superior serenity of an altar of its own, three escritoires supporting, among peonies and peacock feathers and pink candles, between a Holy Family of Tiepolo and a Mary Magdalen attributed to Lucas Cranach, the lady's coat of arms embroidered on a shield of amaranthine plush.

No matter, it was with one voice that the town proclaimed

England's victory—brutal victory that it was, a tawdry triumph of impressionist paganism to be dearly paid for in the next world.

Whereas the altar of the Hôtel de France—without my discussing the pertinence of its charming display of non-spinning lilies—was destined to be the setting for a more aesthetic second edition of the Miracle of the Roses.

Yes, the legendary Miracle of the Roses!

Or so it was at least in the eyes of her who was its heroine, a touching and symbolical creature, snatched away too early from the affection of her family and the dilettantism of her friends.

On the main square (the principal station of the Corpus Christi procession, where the Hôtel d'Angleterre and the Hôtel de France are renewing the painful rivalries of Waterloo and the Grand-Prix) already a few flashy foreigners, instead of cultivating their immortal souls and so forth, are lounging about with simple townspeople.

How pretty it all is in the broad June sun, but ah, look! A creature of twilight has just come upon the scene.

"Are you comfortable there, Ruth?"

"Yes, Patrick."

Under a colonnade at the hotel entrance, the young invalid reclines primly on her chaise lounge, her brother Patrick covers her with plaids while a gold-buttoned porter, whose obsequiousness merits a slap in the face, arranges a folding screen on her left.

Patrick sits down at his sister's side. He holds her handkerchief diaphanous as perfume, her box of orange cachou, her fan, that ironic and sad caprice of the last hour, her flask of real musk, that last consolation of the dying. He holds these tragic stage properties of his sister's constantly at the service of her every glance, a glance already reinitiated in the original heights out there beyond life (life, that diet of oblivion), a glance busy at the moment in meditating on the light and shadow of hands with tragic pearl-tipped fingers—her own.

Ruth has never been married or betrothed, but a wedding ring, terribly thin, of course, graces the ring finger on one pearl-tipped hand—a further note of mystery.

O ideal deathbed maiden, too soon snatched away from the dilettantism of her friends, in her pleated iron-gray gown, her fur cape on her shoulders, and her high lace collar held by a thin gold coin stamped with three fleur-de-lys. Hair of red amber piled up on her forehead and elaborately braided in gentle coils on her fair neck, in the style of Julia Mammea; bewildered eyes, virtuous but wild; a greedy but bloodless little mouth, an expression whose loveliness is a little late in developing! A little late indeed in developing, for how could this waxen tint ever redden again in a lover's quarrel?

She speaks, probably just to hear her voice once more.

"The noise of that torrent will kill me . . ."

She refers, of course, to the waterfall there beside the hotel.

"Come now, Ruth, don't give yourself ideas."

To brighten her spirits, she fumbles among the pale tea roses (the doctor has forbidden her the blood-red variety) scattered on her black and white checkerboard rug. Then she ends as always by saying, although with a look of such delicate martyrdom that it dispels every suspicion of pose!

"Weak, Patrick, weak as a sachet that has lost its scent . . ."

They are brother and sister, but of different, very different, mothers. He is four years younger than she, a youth as noble as one of the fir trees of his native land. They have been living for the past two months in a secluded wing of the hotel.

"Weak, Patrick, weak as a sachet . . ."

Too pure to live, too nervous merely to scrape along, and too diamondlike to be scratched by existence, the inviolable Ruth like a sachet indeed empties herself from one winter resort to another, always following the sun, that lover of putrefaction, the graveyard, and the virgin waxdoll. . .

Last year saw the tubercular beauty in India, at Darjeeling, and it was there that the spice of hallucination was added to her consumption. Although already withdrawn from the conflicts of this low bloodthirsty world, she found herself the only witness of a suicide one moonlit night in a garden. The only witness and, very much in spite of herself, the cause. And since that time in the thin blood coughed up from her own lungs, she thinks she beholds the red passionate blood of that enigmatical suicide; and at the sight of it so deeply imbued with concise and poignant things, she grows delirious.

Consumptive and delirious: no matter what may lie at the heart of all this romancing, the young lady is not here for long, as the servants express it in the kitchen and basement of the hotel; for there is no mercy below stairs.

And so, as in a dream that interrupts for a season or two his own travels and his own heroic development, the good Patrick follows with a fatalist's eye the dying, dying auroras of the fevered spots on his sister's cheeks, and the blood-red crescents in her handkerchief. He exists only to lean over her eyes, sometimes as bright as those of the wild Atlantic sea bird, sometimes lost in a coal-tar mist, to lean over the veins of her temples, blue as flashes of heat lightning, to serve her at table, to take her walking, to bring her every morning a pretty bouquet, never containing a black marigold, to show her pictures, play her little Norwegian pieces from an album of Kjerulf, to read to her in a clear fresh voice.

Now as they await the procession, to keep her mind off the vulgar gaping creatures who have gathered at the foot of the stair, Patrick is reading his sister the last pages of *Séraphita*.

"Like a white dove, a soul came to rest for a moment on this body . . ."

"What silly description," says Ruth. "No, it belongs decidedly to the low syrupy seraphic, that effort. It smells of Geneva where it was written. And this messenger of light with sword and helmet! Poor, poor Séraphita! No, Balzac with that bullneck of his could never have been your brother."

And Ruth with sublime reserve continues to fumble with one hand among the tea roses scattered over the black and white checkerboard of her rug, while the other plays with a strange enamel medallion whose esoteric presence seems to padlock her sexless breast.

Strange, strange, the enamel medallion she caresses on her sexless breast! Pray, let us draw near it. It is a relief of a barbarous and futuristic sort: the enormous and splendid eye of a peacock's tail reposing under a human eyelid, the whole encircled by bloodless cabochons. One May afternoon, in the Bois, a poor devil whom Ruth had noticed for some time always in her path leapt from behind the shrubbery, followed her carriage, and hurling this medallion at her feet, said in a perfectly natural voice:

"For you alone, and you must know that the day you put it aside, I shall leave this life."

When she came into a drawing room one evening later, a gentleman fainted dead away at the sight of her. After he recovered, the gentleman stammered that he had not fainted because of her, but because of the enamel medallion on her breast. He begged her to let him have it for his collection. Ruth told him why she was obliged to refuse, and described the poor madman as best she could. The collector searched for him, failed to find him, and promptly went into a decline. One day he came to Ruth's house, and surrendered to the vastness of nature the poor soul of one who loved only artificial things.

And so the secret is out! Ruth, this charming dying creature, through the incomprehensible workings of fate, spends her life spreading suicide on her way, along the stations of the cross.

Ruth had operated in Biarritz before adding her note of sadness to this little spa; and despite her horror of blood, had asked to see a bullfight at San Sebastian.

Ruth and her imperturbable brother were sitting in the governor's box above the bull's entrance. Ah, how excited she was in her loose gown of tea-colored muslin, without folds or flounces, hastily thrown together in the devil-may-care fashion of a shroud, in order not to affront, it seemed, by too exaggerated a cut or too resistant a finish, the indefensible and unmodish dissolution of the lady who was to wear it!

The bestial blood that flowed there, slowly drunk by the sand of the arena, supplanted that of her usual nightmare.

Quietly and with no feeling of nausea she had already exulted over the sight of six jades disemboweled, four bulls gashed and finally run through, and two thrown *banderilleros*, one gored in the thigh. She always held back the governor's arm when the entire ring signaled to him, with a thousand waving handkerchiefs, to wave his own and put an end to the massacre of the *picadores'* horses and call out the *banderilleros*.

"Oh, not yet, *señor presidente*, the next engagement will be the most beautiful . . ."

With the fifth bull, a volley of jeers broke over the weak *señor presidente*. Two horses, in their death agony, lay in each other's embrace waiting to be dispatched. Two others were dragged away, their guts streaming to the ground. Finally, at a signal, the heavy *picadores* dressed in yellow had withdrawn, leaving the bull silent and ready to face the *banderillero*, who stood waiting with his two beribboned javelins. He was bleeding, the poor bull, from the many wounds he had received (superficial scratches intended to exasperate rather than weaken him). He bounded, then turned, and went back to sniff the limp masses of the two wounded horses and turn them over with his little horns. He sat down in front of them like a brotherly sentinel and laid his forehead against them as if he were trying to understand. In vain the *banderillero* called to him, teased him, and even hurled his black-tasseled cap at his feet. The bull just went on trying to understand, pawing the sand with his angry hoof, completely bewildered by this enclosed field of brilliant colors and clamoring people where all he could do was rip open blindfolded horses and rush at floating red rags.

A *capador* jumped over the wall and threw a collapsed goatskin bottle in his face. The spectators applauded.

And then suddenly before those twenty thousand fans fluttering patiently under a wide splendid sky, the beast stretched his neck unmistakably toward Ruth, as if she alone were the cause of all this cruelty. Far from his native pastures he began to utter cries so superhumanly distressing (cries of such genius, really) that there was one of those moments of general shock, as when new religions are founded. And fainting and delirious, the beautiful and inhuman lady of the presidential box—wouldn't you know?—was carried out.

And Ruth took up again her blood-curdling refrain:

"Blood, blood . . . there, on the grass; all the perfumes of Arabia . . ."

And naturally with Ruth on the scene, the slaughter of bulls and horses had to come to a strange end that day! This *señor presidente,* who had never laid eyes on our young and symbolical heroine before, this peculiar creole gentleman with his malarial face and gold-rimmed spectacles, who had remained so impassive and composed before the jeering throng, killed himself that very evening. He bequeathed to Ruth some of the knick-knacks he had collected in the colonies during those consular exiles that had made his strange weary soul what it was. He left also an enigmatical but noble letter that fortunately Patrick succeeded in intercepting. Patrick had of course by this time given up trying to make any sense of this epidemic of bizarre scenes.

And who indeed could, unless it is the Lord in Heaven?

—— III ——

When the bells had caught their breath, they struck one more resounding blow in the bosom of nature that hasn't brains enough to know whether it is "natural" or "naturalized," but will always manage somehow to make both ends meet.

The Procession of the Lord in Heaven could be heard approaching. There was a flourish of trumpets, and it appeared.

First two choirboys in red carrying the censer and the old silver cross in the customary bored fashion.

Then, stamping like a drove of cattle, schoolboys filed past, two by two, dressed in their Sunday best by poor mamas who had outdone themselves. With their hymnbooks open in their hats, they dragged their litany slowly toward the bushy acacias of the Promenade. The first two, clearly the sons of influential citizens, hoisted a worn silk banner, the tassels of which were held by two sons of less influential citizens. The father of one of them rushed forth from the crowd, and with proper parish pride adjusted the careful parting in his darling Eliacin's hair with his small brush. The last four members of the flock, tall and rather pale in their black communion suits, bore on their shoulders the shafts of a Pietà in the style of the rue Saint-Sulpice. Four precentors in discolored top hats, with glaring gloves and brilliant sashes, kept an eye on everything, strutting about like sergeants at arms.

Then came some little girls, looking like barley-sugar angels, in white frocks with blue sashes, their curls wreathed with lilies of the valley, their bare arms carrying baskets of petals to strew in their path, while well-heeled matrons shaded them with maternal umbrellas.

Then boarding-school girls, in an odd array of simple dresses, singing softly.

Then a group of white-gowned virgins, winners of the Rose, some congregation of the Children of Mary, looking exceedingly proper with their wreaths and gloves, carrying a banner here and there, and here and there a plaster statue, and other vague relics.

Dressed in white, too, a procession of first communicants in long pleated veils with lowered eyes, hands touching in a pious point, murmuring together things they had learned by heart (Ah! when one's heart is in such things! . . .)

Then on the heels of the fire brigade came the band, advancing in close formation. The band was composed of ham-smoked peasants in frock coats and top hats; brasses dented in homeward journeys from wedding dances, clarinets in the style of Jocrisse at the fair, a bruised bass drum in slings, and dog-eared music fastened to their instruments. At the moment they were in the act of dismembering the Wedding March from Mendelssohn's *Midsummer Night's Dream.*

After the band, four carefully selected flower girls came by, scattering rose petals from their baskets. And finally, on the shoulders of four hefty fellows, the gold-fringed pink canopy sheltering the ecclesiastic who was to officiate. Pompous to behold from without but paralyzed from within, he held out to the faithful along the way the legendary monstrance of the Most Holy Sacrament.

And the canopy came to a stop before the altar of the Hôtel de France!

O hushed steps of edifying unction, silence in the full light of day, bell sounding sacred and shrill at the moment of elevation, censer swinging as during mass! The Holy Sacrament was obviously the high point of the procession.

The gentlemen had removed their hats, a number of ladies had knelt on the edge of the pavement. No elegant sceptic said a word.

O silence in the full light of day, bell sounding sacred and shrill at the moment of elevation, censers raised through clouds of homage! Everybody was in heaven.

But for Ruth, the unfortunate and symbolical heroine I have created, this tantalizing silence, this bell as relentless and shrill as the bells on Judgment Day, must surely record that grief of griefs in those unjust valleys beyond the grave where the Suicide wanders, the Suicide who loved too much, the Suicide with the hole in his head.

She unclasps her feverishly devout hands, and clutching her brother's arm, sets about moaning again from the depths of her somnambulistic limbo.

"Blood, blood, there on the grass! . . . All the perfumes of

Arabia . . . O Patrick, if I only knew why! . . . Why I should be chosen rather than another in this wide world where our sex is in the majority?"

Patrick could cry out once and for all in front of everybody: "You began it!" But no, he caresses her hands, gently gives her the smelling salts, and waits quietly, although he can already feel her growing faint.

The Priest who bears the Holy Sacrament turns noticeably toward the wealthy young invalid for a moment, and favors her with a remote movement of his consecrated lips.

And at the same moment a little girl is thrust forward through the crowd by a tense and beaming young man. Red with shame, as if obeying some dreadful command, she climbs the steps and scatters all the roses in her basket around the chaise longue of the fainting girl. The child almost loses her balance as she goes back down.

There are moments in this life that are absolutely heart-rending, heart-rending for all classes of society. This was not one of them, but there are such moments and the exception only confirms the rule.

The procession again got under way. The Holy Sacrament now went on to cense the Hôtel d'Angleterre's hysterical rococo polychrome Saint Theresa, before censing in turn the armed altar of the Duchess H. While the hymns began again at the head, the tail of the procession filed past.

It filed past, the tail of the procession. First, the household of the fallen queen; then in two columns, a whole senate of citizens, hats in hand, marked by the indelible stigmata of their callings, from apoplectic butchers to pale pastry cooks. Then bowed and wrinkled peasants with unsightly skulls, their caps in their hands. A few had crutches, while others walked alone, reciting their prayers. Then came the Sisters of Charity, with long flowing sleeves, their winged headdresses quivering like Holy Ghosts hideously starched by a religion that had taken flight on its own ceremonies. Then a few ladies with parasols, and some servant girls. Then some peasant women with old-fashioned shawls and sunburned goitres. At intervals someone was telling his beads while his neighbors murmured the responses.

And the Corpus Christi procession ended by ending, stupidly lopped off by a timid group of servant girls.

And the general public poured after them, amid the dust and trampled flowers, toward their *déjeuners à la carte*.

In the meantime, while they are taking down the altar . . .

All good things come to an end!

Ruth revives, and looks about in a state of exultation, one hand on the enamel plaque that locks her sexless breast, the other pointing around her:

"O Patrick, Patrick! Look at the roses in its place! No more blood, but roses of a blood redeemed forever! Oh, give me one to touch . . ."

"Yes, it's really true!" says Patrick without thinking, so instinctively tender, and wholly his sister's. "Oh, indeed, blood changed into roses! . . ."

"Then he is saved, Patrick?"

"He is saved."

She fills her hands with petals and sinks her face in them, sobbing.

"Oh, the poor creature. Now I won't have to worry about him any more."

All of which ends up in a coughing fit that must be treated with the same old benzoin syrup.

And so, thanks to the roses, roses so appropriately scattered at such a happy moment by a nameless little girl, Ruth was exorcised of her hallucinations, and from that day on could devote herself fully and purely to her consumption, whose record she again took up with a pen dipped in a blue-flowered copy of a Delft inkwell.

Needless to say she never knew that the very evening of this same Corpus Christi Day, the brother of the little girl with the basket of miraculous roses also killed himself for her sake, in a hotel room with no other witness to the state of his poor heart than the Lord in Heaven.

But the Miracle of the Roses was worked in all the glory of blood and roses. Hallelujah!

LOHENGRIN, SON OF PARSIFAL

Beside his dear slumbering body, how many long nights I have watched, seeking to discover why he wanted so to escape from reality.

—A. Rimbaud

Oh, how impossible to recapture, even in one's imagination, the evenings devoted to the Great Sacrifices! . . .

Naturally, for the degradation of the Vestal Elsa, they had chosen the rising of the implacable and Divine First Full Moon, and as setting for the ceremony, the square in front of the Cathedral of Our Lady, with all the bells tolling *Nox Irae* out over the everlasting sea, calm as it always is on fine evenings.

On two facing platforms hung with inviolable white linen are seated the White Council and the Corporation of Vestals; between these two institutions in a semicircle stand a whispering congregation, whose blue, green, gray eyes are glazed by waiting before the sea, overpowering as it always is on fine evenings.

It is still broad daylight; and no clement evening breeze teases the brief flames of the altar candles.

What can be about to take place?

Goodness, how white and barbaric all this seems now, on the edge of the solemn, deep basin of the sea! And, oh, how remote from my native village! . . .

Now then, upon the enchanted horizon Our Lady is about to make her appearance.

Ah, indeed, it is—the lovely old-gold full moon, bewildered, hallucinatory, palpable and round! So near it is that one might mistake it for a work of humankind, some aerostatic experiment of modern times. (Yes, a moon as simple in its swollen perfection as a rising balloon!)

And, as always, it casts a chill.

And, as always, the chalky façades of the square with their bal-
conies hung with rented shrouds and the rose window of the
Basilica of Silence, in its sepulchral efflorescence, take on an interesting pallor; and amid this bright new enchantment the brief
yellow flames of the altar candles seem but poor family jewels.

Hail, Queen of Lilies!

Sacrament of Lethe! Transfiguring Mirror!

Mecca of polar Sterilities!

There, above the Ciborium-Ocean, the fully bruised, poorly cau-
terized Eucharist!

And, on the horizon, the waves, until then enchanted with
calm, are now beginning to carry out in her direction a gentle
rocking, markedly rocking movement, as if begging her to let herself sink away for a bit, all white, this night, to be rocked to sleep
with dark delight.

The bells have given out.

And the crowd—men, women, children, old crones in a thin,
high-pitched soprano chorus—begin to shriek the *Stabat* of Pales-
trina, but in an infinitely expurgated version.

And, at this shrill signal, the Aviary-Lighthouse of the Goddess
releases its sacred gulls.

Ah, off they fly, mewing wildly, like bird-moths toward the
Full Moon, and flutter about her face; then, after these prelimi-
nary devotions, off on little fishing jaunts as is their custom on
fine evenings.

Intoxicated by these preludes, the spectators in their white vest-
ments are seated.

What silence! . . .

The eldest High Priest of Selene has risen; in the polar silence
he censes three times the path of the Full Moon; then intones:

"My Sisters, how these evenings enhance your beauty!

"Across the impassable lagoons of the sea, the Immaculately
Conceived (the only one!) now makes her way toward us. Hail
to Thee, Virgin of the Night, O icy expanse, may Thy name be

honored among women, to whom Thou givest the silken distinc-
tion of their breasts, making them to swell with the necessary
milk."

The Vestals rise, and all together, except for the last row of
novices, who are still committed to silence, repeat the invocation;
and then all (in three movements, but not without a certain quite
excusable coquettish languor) throw back their pale cashmere
shawls, undo their linen wimples, and exhibit to the beneficent
planet their young breasts like oh, so many eucharistic wafers, so
many aspiring moons. And the novices shiver a little to feel their
almond nipples harden under the holy beams come from so far
across the impassable lagoons of the sea.

But one among them, standing somewhat apart in the first row,
has taken no part in this charming manifestation, even to the ex-
tent of lowering her head toward her condemned breast.

The High Priest, as he watches her, continues all the more
firmly:

"O almond nipples, seals of maternity, suck up the effluvia of
the Holy Sacrament which has risen on the sea, having come to
make its round in your dormitories. For you are still its virgins,
worthy of maintaining its Mysteries, of guarding its filters and its
incantatory formulae, worthy of blessing the wedding bread. Hail,
then, to the Virginal Lighthouse, to the Polar Lookout, to the
Labarum of Modern Societies!"

He sits back down.

The Vicar of Diana-Artemis rises, dorically draped, pale as the
statue of the Holy Father of the Faithful.

"Elsa! Elsa! Elsa!" he intones three times in his perfect sectarian
voice.

The Vestal, standing apart in the first row, a little woman with
her breasts still hidden with shame, advances on the platform, with
lowered head and a downright injured air.

"Elsa, sworn Vestal, guardian of the Mysteries, the filters, the
formulae, and the wheat for the wedding bread, what have you

done with the key to your repertory? Ah, your breasts know a caress other than the distant one of the moon; your flesh has been inoculated with a science other than that of the cult; profane hands have unfastened your girdle and broken the seal of your delicate solitude. What, pray tell, have you to say for yourself?"

Elsa replies with angelic clarity: "I believe that I am innocent. O cruel mistakes!"—and in a low voice, to herself, "Good Lord, what a lot of silly talk!"

The members of the White Council, dismissing her plea with a wave of their hands, proceed.

And the Confessor of Hecate bobs up and unrolls the parchment of indictment.

"On the night of . . . " etc., etc.

(Nothing but suspicions on the whole, and pointedly vulgar suspicions at that.)

". . . The mere fact of being publicly suspected makes her unworthy of the cult. Widow Elsa, forget that you were a Vestal! Forget for ever and ever the Mysteries, the filters, the formulae, and the yeast for the matrimonial bread. Now, widow Elsa, for one last time contemplate the Goddess; for, according to ritual, if, after being summoned three times, your fiancé does not present himself to take you unto him, we will burn out your lovely eyes, touching them as delicately as possible with the Aerolite of Sacrilege which came to us on the first moon of the Hegira, and rests, as you well know, wrapped in linen in the vault of the Goddess at the heart of the Basilica of Silence.—Ladies and gentlemen, we shall now make the three customary summonses."

And everyone can see that Elsa does not even bother to glance at the crowd, from the midst of which it is quite clear she expects no knight to emerge.

The Matrons in ribboned caps patterned on the headdress of the Sphinx lead her down from the platform, remove her pale cashmere, her linen wimple, and her emblematic pearls. The pearls they tie up in the wimple and cashmere, and the entire package consigned to a leaden box is, in a thrilling succession of symbolic gestures, committed to the waves, to sink down toward the submarine graveyards.

Which leaves Elsa face to face with the good people in her rôle of promised bride. Oh, promised and promising creature in her long pale gown starred from head to foot with peacock's eyes (black, blue, green and gold, which are familiar to all of us, but of which it is pleasant to be reminded), her shoulders bare, her arms left angelically to their nudity, with her waist bound just below her young breasts by a wide blue sash from which hangs a peacock feather with an even more magnificent eye, and over this central jeweled eye the poor thing has modestly crossed her little hands in their long blue mittens. But her eyes remain still as succulent as mouths, whereas her half-opened mouth has now taken on the full sadness of a fixed eye.

A very perceptible whisper of admiration runs among the women; and, a feeling of solidarity finding them always ready, they intone:

"Happy, happy indeed is he who will lead her across his threshold. What is left of her is adorable; and not yet turned eighteen, if we are not mistaken?"

Elsa does not condescend to confirm this last delectable detail.

A herald advances, lifts upon a paten for the crowd to see the aerolite which is to eat out her lovely succulent eyes, and blows on his ivory horn four blasts to the four points of the compass, and then . . .

"Would you mind blowing a bit more forcefully in the direction of the sea?" Elsa observes.

"She's making fun of us."

"She would just have us dance attendance on her. Let's get on with the sealing of her eyes!"

"I wish to have nothing to reproach myself with," declares the High Priest: "Herald, comply with her request and blow a bit more forcefully in the direction of the sea!"

The herald blows a ridiculously loud blast in the obvious direction of the sea. Then he roars:

"If any man wishes to take Elsa, castoff Vestal, for his lawfully wedded wife, let him advance at once and swear to do so in a loud and intelligible voice!"

Elsa does not deign to let the pupil of her eye stray toward the crowd; turning her back on the ceremony, she seems to inspect the thoroughly unknown horizon of the sea.

And no one says a word . . . Many mothers have put their sons under lock and key today; and besides she is much too proud!—a situation that hardly bodes well for the future.

The two other summonses remain unanswered.

"Adjudicated!"

Elsa rushes forward. "Oh," she says, "will someone first let me have a mirror?"

A young man emerges from the crowd and goes over to present the condemned with a pocket mirror. "Could you love me?" he whispers. "Could you follow me about everywhere with those adoring eyes, if . . ."

"No, that's not necessary; thank you."

And then she gazes admiringly at herself in the mirror. And, instead of giving herself over to elegies on the fate of her eyes, she arranges her coiffure, smooths the arches of her celebrated eyebrows, and arranges and rearranges her hair.

(What total absence of moral sense!)

"Now, I hope that I may be allowed to address a bit of a prayer to the Moon, the Mistress of us all?"

Without waiting for further deliberation on the subject, Elsa kneels on the sand of the shore. And then, extending her little blue-gloved hands toward the enchanted horizon of the sea, she begins to intone:

"Brave Knight who appeared to me that fatal and memorable evening, riding a great shining swan!

"Will you abandon your slave? As you well know, fatal Knight, my succulent eyes under their celebrated brows and my sad mouth are yours to command, and you know that I will follow you everywhere with my wild gaze.

"Ah, my flesh is still faint and trembling from your vision; and"—placing her hand upon her heart—"the little crater of my heart still flames from it, and from it I have discovered within myself a whole assortment of treasures. For your noble whim, you know, will constitute my shame.

"Lovely Knight, I have not yet turned eighteen. Listen, if you come to claim me, you will certainly not regret it. Sound the angelus! The Shulamite am I, whose modesty is but that of a flower . . ."

She leans forward a moment, her hand before her eyes, scrutinizing the enchanted horizon; then, drawing out her words, continues:

"Yes, I am indeed yours to command, Prince Charming. And, believe me, I shall be able to knit you the mesh of many a new suit of armor.

"And, I must say, the loveliness of my gown will cause your starved papillae to open. . . . And the moons of my elbows, glistening like falling larks, ah . . .

"Will my adorable Knight leave me to grow old, a blind outcast, in this bourgeois society? I am beautiful, beautiful—a veritable Vision incarnate!

"Oh, I understand you already! I shall follow you everywhere with my wild gaze. And I shall attach myself so completely to the light of your brow that I shall never grow old; yes, I shall be so firmly mounted in your furrow of light that I shall be as a little diamond that age can never cut!

"Ah, but no. I am but one of the weaker sex, and all I shall be able to do is water your crystal armor every morning with my tears! . . ."

She turns toward the Executioner, whose heart is encased in a substance three times as hard as stone.

"I tell you he *will* come! He promised me; and you will see for once in your life what I mean by a handsome man. Ah, here he is! Here he is! Judge for yourself!"

The gulls fly off, mewing distressfully, toward the aviary-dormitories of the Lighthouse.

O lovely evening . . .

Up from the horizon, over the smooth resigned waves, in the enchantment of the spreading Full Moon, a great luminous swan advances majestically with its neck curving like a prow into the water; astride it a youth in shining armor, swelling with incredible confidence, extends his arms toward the Beach-Tribunal!

And the executioners are immediately changed into gaping boobies, flocking down to the sand around poor bewildered Elsa, who can hardly get out the words: "Don't jostle so! Don't you see that you're rumpling my gown!"

And the booby-executioners exclaim:

"Who then is this true knight coming over the seas, melodious with bravura, free as the mountain peaks, his pink brow carunculated with Faith? What a joyous occasion! Elsa, we wish you happiness, my dear, and with no mental reservations; you may certainly expect handsome offspring. And how he rides that seraphic bird, that avalanche become a swan! Oh, it must be none other than Endymion himself, Diana's little man. And the sound of his voice must indeed be . . . providential!"

He glides in, ever increasing in stature, magical, maintaining his pose, sure of everything!

How rich and refined his family must be! And, oh, in what magical groves are they now taking their ices. Is it far, so far as that? . . . Has he been traveling long?

Here he is! Yes, it is He! What woman anywhere could find him mentally incompatible?

The gentle Knight has set foot on the shore. But before turning to other matters, he pets the prowlike neck of his lovely taciturn and quite heraldic swan, and says:

"Farewell and many thanks, my handsome swan-chariot, fly back toward that horizon now blocked by the Full Moon, pass through the torrents of stars, round the cape of the Sun, and sail back between the banks curdled by the galaxies of the Milky Way, toward the peerless lake of the Holy Grail; go, my sweet!"

The swan spreads its wings, and lifting itself straight up with a wholly unprecedented and imposing vibration, it scuds along at full sail and soon disappears completely beyond the Moon.

Oh, what a sublime way to burn your bridges behind you, noble fiancé!

When the swan has duly been lost to sight, there is an icy and rather awkward silence. The Knight advances without a sign of intimidation, and remarks:

"I am not Endymion; I come straight from the Holy Grail. Parsifal is my father; of my mother I know nothing. I am Lohengrin, Knight-Errant, lily of future crusades for the Emancipation of Woman. In the meantime, I was far too unhappy working in my father's office. (I am slightly hypochondriacal by nature.) I have come to wed the lovely swan-throated Elsa, who dwells among you. Where is her mother, pray tell, that I may speak to her?"

"Like all Vestals, Elsa is an orphan," proclaims the herald.

"Really! Oh, here she is, I recognize her at once! Where were you hiding? What lovely peacock feathers! Who gave them to you? At dawn tomorrow I'll explain their significance to you! And how . . . beautiful your eyes are! And how—perfect—is your entire person!"

They fall at each other's knees—simultaneously, and, alas, quite fatally.

"Good Knight, all that I am and all that I hope to be, and all that my past involves, I lay at your feet. This is as you expected; and I am not one to go back on my word."

"Elsa, no, no, you are too precious to prostrate yourself like that!—What a divine human specimen! Do get up!"

"I'm really not bad to look upon; but you will teach me to know myself intimately. I am so easy to train; may I address you in a more familiar manner?"

"O my little Virgin Queen of the May!"

"You don't mean it!"

Now let the nuptial tocsins sound, the bells, all the bells, of the City. Let the bells of lovely Sundays ring out over the tranquil provinces! Happiness of clean linen, which makes one feel as if one had not been soiled all week! Proper happiness of little school-girls in their Sunday finery passing through the great portal of the Cathedral! Bells! Bells! Some young, some restless, some sacred, but all alternating without bickering in a single hymn to the future. And what they are saying is clear, is it not? "The Communion cloth has been laid! Here is the wafer. Say to yourselves: 'This is my flesh and blood!' "

The three wretched priests raise their overstuffed and smoking censers three times in the direction of the Full Moon, which is completely topaz and utterly calm in the midst of these strange fetishist manifestations.

And everyone files slowly up to the Temple, toward the illuminated nuptial rood-screens, while the great organs resound with *Hosannah's* and *Crescite et multiplicamini's*.

"Do you know Latin?" asks Elsa.

"A bit; and you?"

"Oh, I'm not such a blue stocking as all that—I'm just an ordinary young lady! And besides, Latinate words are a menace to one's modesty, or so I seem to have read in an old almanac . . ."

They kneel before the altar draped in inviolable linen beneath a canopy blazing with oriflammes flickering in the happy gusts of the great organ.

The ceremony begins . . . and unfolds with an array of holy this and that . . .

The golden doors of the Tabernacle spring open like the capsules of plants, and disclose the monstrance with its moon-shaped paten, unswathed in linen, and presented upon a manutergium.

The two take Communion from it distractedly without stealing glances at each other.

"Oh," exclaims Lohengrin, "I am suffocating under your gaze!" With long lustral tears he wets the linen of the altar.

"You will see how amiable I am," she assures him in a low voice. "But your teeth are chattering! Don't take it all so seriously! I don't believe in any of this; my word, I don't consider that Moon of theirs anything but a sort of cruel stepmother, a kind of hairless idol for foolish old people."

"No, but the trouble is those organs . . ."

"Ah, but you know I really love music!"

The sopranos in the organ lofts are shrieking:

"Enamored orphans, the meadows of youth await your failing thighs. Staggering and bleating out the ritornelli of your hearts' nocturnal orioles, and whipping yourselves with carefully chosen stamens, be drawn hypnotically toward the moon during sowing-time, and caress one another afterward in the oddest way in order to release your night-flying butterflies from their cocoons! For all the rest is nothing but Desire."

Finally while the organ unwinds the thread of a fugue with the familiar theme "It is growing late," the congregation files out in somewhat less orderly fashion than it had entered, torn as it is by so many conflicting emotions.

The night will probably be warm. The roofs, the shore, the city, and the country sleep frozen beneath the moon; the grassy terraces of the sea shimmer in floods of gala moonlight; space is sprinkled with an invisible, magical manna.

The dazzling sacrament is at its zenith! And one would almost like to detach the gondolas and go out there on the water-mirror to capture with a net the motionless image of such a dazzling sacrament. . . .

And presenting this spectacle to them with a wave of the hand, the Council shouts to the couple the traditional witticism in front of this window display of white: "Come, children! The table is laid and your fortune made."

> Oh, the table is laid
> For Christian lover and maid!
> Wedding party, be gone from here!
> Off to your homes, each one of you.
> Nice young girls in need of a beau,
> May God next year answer your prayers!

The choruses die away—leaving these children, poor things, all to themselves.

— II —

The Nuptial Villa, nestling in a little bay in an artificial garden area of the coast, is under the jurisdiction of the Minister of Cults. It is free of charge to newlyweds but for the first week of their honeymoon only; no midwife is therefore in residence.

The couple thought it was quite near, since they could see so clearly the marvelous solitary silver poplar that marked the entrance. But, thanks to the ingenious windings of the flower-bordered paths, it took several quarters of an hour, and several quarters of an hour of joyous conversation before they could hear the palpitation of the marvelous poplar on the threshold.

Several quarters of an hour of loving conversation or of simply plunging forward arm-in-arm, trembling and ecstatic.

"Dear Knight, how lovely the moonlight shines on your strange crystal armor!"

"Doesn't it? And how elevating it is for the soul! . . ."

"And what effect does it have on my beauty?"

"The coils of your dark hair are made no less warm by it."

"And my heart matches my hair. But why do you speak to me so formally now?"

"Ah, because now you are becoming somebody, somebody to be reckoned with right away."

"Indeed! But short reckonings make long friendships."

"How enchanting are the borders of these discouraging paths!"

The moonlight is so extreme that the birds in their nests chatter gaily away and the anthills proceed with their diurnal labors.

Here, at last, without a doubt, is the sublime nuptial poplar, all its frail silver leaves trembling in this polar enchantment against a background of glacial ultramarine sky.

Lohengrin suddenly drops his companion's arm and kneels on the ground.

"Oh," he says, "I thought that I was Lohengrin, the lily become a man. But how you surpass me, O glorious poplar; growing there where you were born; your slightest branches sweep in unanimity toward the Empyrean, and the elusive silver of your foliage whispers with unchanging purity on the threshold of this Nuptial Villa, watching the couples come and go week after week."

"Let's go in! Let's go in! We're home at last!" sings Elsa as she claps her hands.

They venture in, and immediately, without hesitating, consumed with a silent uneasiness, their feet irritated by the lukewarm gravel, they hurry off toward what seem to be approaching waterfalls—through still more discouraging labyrinths of yew trees clipped into corridors and through strangely plastic stratifications, past the lonely plip-plop of balsam-and-myrrh-scented opaline fountains in the midst of circular marble terraces where white peacocks strut, trailing their immaculate feathers in the moonlight.

And these were indeed waterfalls that they had heard, a circle of eternal waterfalls surrounding a pool whose translucent water, hardly a foot deep, offers up the shining mica of its pure white sand to lunar enchantment.

Ah, now they throw off the crystal armor and the trailing gown starred with peacock's eyes; in Edenlike nakedness they enter the water giggling and lie weakly down in the middle as if beneath ideal coverlets; leaning on one elbow, they begin to chat a bit to regain their senses.

They steal glances at each other.

Lohengrin, haughty youth, has one leg tucked under the other as if perched on a sofa.

Elsa, as she stretches out beneath the moon, is thin and all her lines are hard and awkward—how I hate those soft inflections that are bound to flow past satiety right into decay!—proud-hipped, with her legs fit to grip a tough stallion, her bosom held upright, unashamed of the two breasts with so little chubbiness to them that they could easily fit beneath two saucers.

Resting on one elbow in water up to her throat, Elsa undoes her hair and lets it trail floating on the water around her tilting face, which seems then for a moment, amid these water weeds and balanced on the frail stem of her neck, like some inhuman lacustrine flower.

Having achieved the desired effect, Elsa shakes herself:

"Ah, I must say I had had enough of those platonic cults and that cloistered life. Don't you find me a bit crumbly like old parchment? What would you say to a little run over the green, my dear?"

"As you like."

"Ah, you don't love me. Which is just as I expected. The whole thing was too beautiful from the start!"

"But yes, I do love you. I love you to excess! . . ."

He extends his arm and gives her a cordial handshake; then recovering himself:

"Come, tell me quickly, quickly a little about your life."

"But my dear, I haven't lived at all . . . not until tonight. (You know that I've not yet turned eighteen, don't you?) I've dreamed of this and that, of you, Gentle Knight, that's about all."

"And, of course, you know what everything is all about. Why don't you answer? Have the anatomical plates of human destiny never passed before your eyes? . . ."

"Oh, you'll be sorry all your life for having said that to me!"

"But what have I said? I have only alluded to things that are very natural and extremely delightful, after all! . . . Ah they will always have the last word," sighs Lohengrin, gazing off into space.

He rises; she rises, taking hold, in a graceful and conjugal fashion, of his arm.

"But perhaps I am getting you wet," she says.

"Oh, don't worry about anything like that."

They take a turn around the pool, stopping here and there, at the loveliest of the waterfalls, to break the shimmering surface with the tip of a toe, and let the water slip madly cold between their fingers. And Elsa uses this as a pretext for sinking against the torso of her darling. And he calms her, not with banal kisses, but with heartfelt words.

For the sake of peace and quiet, they go sit down on one of the lushly swarded banks.

"How do you feel now?" asks Lohengrin.

"And how should I feel?"

"Oh, did you hear an owl hoot somewhere off there?"

"And, oh, all around us this sound of germination? What a night it is! . . ."

"Come now," the strange Knight muses to himself: "No absolute, only compromises. Anything goes. Nothing surprises."

And he ventures to caress her rather oddly. Then he comes out with this reflection: "This Nuptial Villa reeks of the tomb."

"We are all mortal," she replies in a decidedly conciliatory voice.

Finally he whispers for them both, "Suppose we go back in?"

The Full Moon is high, very high now, tumefied and octopus-colored.

They hear through the night, replete with its simplified solutions, only the decrepit rasping of frogs.

"But look, what are those structures down there? Ah, yes, it seems that there is a stone carved with symbols and with bits of advice . . ."

"Come, come, you'll take cold."

They go back in without speaking, he overwhelmed by transcendental responsibilities, she quite in her element.

He muses:

> No Absolute
> Only compromises;
> Anything goes;
> Nothing surprises.

She muses:

> A nest all furnished
> By some devoted squire,
> Winds all subdued,
> With nights by the fire;
> Nothing transitory,
> Not a fuss, not a scene,
> Life's really nice and clean
> When you know the whole story.

They go back in. The Villa is overgrown with weeds. A façade trimmed with groups of well-espaliered carnations, front steps of pink brick, a balcony of flowered tiles, a thatched roof, a weather vane in the form of a cat that can mew. Resounding corridors, and a plethora of circular staircases. Empty rooms, with names and dates etched with diamonds on the mirrors. Several stories, with the same thing up and down: he was right, it certainly does reek of the tomb.

What a pity really that outside on the lawn it's too cool—and that he is already half-frozen.

Here there are black bearskins and pale pillows in an attic room, the ogival window of which, looking out over the lonely stretches of the sea, has now let in a flood of moonlight.

Is this real life, or a night of hallucination, when all is said and done?

Leaning on one elbow, Lohengrin can see a hint of the shadow

Elsa's lashes cast on her cheek as she nestles up to her neck in the wild furs.

"What are you looking at?" she asks.

"I am reflecting upon the marvelous organization of the human body."

Silence; Elsa raises herself and leans on one elbow.

"May I venture to express myself?"

"Speak."

"But can I really? To you whom I have seen in my dreams, so kind, so eloquent, to you who have brought me here. Can I speak, overwhelmed as I am by the sincerity of all that has happened to me?"

"Ah, the Eternal Feminine. That's what comes, little sister, of having let you grow up on your own, away from humanity. What if we were to set out, on our own, to organize the Eternal Masculine?"

"No sooner said than done! . . ."

"And men of genius! Why do you especially make men of genius suffer? Whence does it come, this instinct that at times confounds the man of thought?"

"I can't say, since it is an instinct . . ."

"Well, you especially make them suffer so they may sweat out their masterpieces! The wild masterpieces of these unfortunate men, you must know, restore with each generation the fortunes of your house so as better to attract the succeeding generation to your daughters."

"What of that, since everybody benefits . . ."

"Oh, good heavens, is she a simple time-honored slave, and one without malice? Is she a transcendental spy? Oh, what if, while buried man rotted quietly away, woman, for her part, went on to a feminine world in which she would be rewarded according to the quality and quantity of dupes whom she had made work for the Ideal on this earth?"

"Whew, how warm it is!"

"You won't answer my misgivings, then?"

"I swear to you that I know nothing about it all, that I love you without any other concern than to please you so that you will have me for your own. And do you think I shan't have my own sorrows to face, my own endless sorrows?"

"Oh, don't cry like that, don't cry! Smile for me, a big smile, now. Come now, sing something for me."

"I only know little girls' songs."

"Fine. I'm listening."

Elsa coughs a little, then begins to sing with tears still in her voice:

> Samson believed in Delilah,
> Dance, dance round the flower pot!
> The prettiest girl in the whole world
> Can only give you what she's got.

"Who taught you that? Don't you know something that's less of an epithalamium?"

With her hand on her heart, her eyes on the tester of the bed, Elsa intones:

> You go away and leave us here,
> You leave us here and go away,
> To plait and unplait our long hair
> And stitch eternal scenes all day.

"No, no! Surely you realize that that isn't very nice! Might you be libidinous, Elsa?"

"I don't know the meaning of the word. But suppose you sing something yourself!"

With exemplary accent, Lohengrin declaims:

> Once there was a King of Thule
> Who, until death did them part,
> Loved a white-winged swan with all his heart,
> One that sailed like a ship on a clear white pool.

When death came down . . .

"Death, death! Oh, I don't want to die! I want to see the world. I want to know all there is to know about Young Women."

He sobs hopelessly into his pillow. She leans over him, and above his feverish temple, with diabolical sincerity, whispers:

"Boy, boy, are you familiar with the voluptuary ceremonies? Behold the sweet almonds of my young breasts, touch my hair and see what a soft and sensual black it is. Examine one of the grass blades of my puberty . . . O ennuiversal resentment! nerve-killing experiences, martyred nights! Love me by degrees, inventory me, massacre me, profane me!"

"You must be out of your mind. You make me fear for your . . ."

"Why, then, do you sulk like that with me? It's really killing after a while!"

"I'm sulking because . . ."

"Why? All I ask is to love you."

"If you must know, it's because I can't stand your slender hips. I can only contemplate wide ones. They at least call to mind quite openly the slavery of childbirth, and that is, after all, what all these lovely things add up to."

"Don't say that to me! What have I done to you?"

"Forgive me, forgive me! Don't cry! I was just being naughty. Oh, but the fact is that I adore straight and narrow hips!"

"Really?"

"Yes, madly. They are the only ones!"

"Well, then?"

"It comes down to this, this is what I abhor in you. There you are with dry, quite antimaternal, hips. And yet you walk with the perpetual swing of a little mammal that has just been unballasted of the half-dozen pounds that brought her to labor. (Why are you laughing?) Yes, I say, with this swing and seemingly quite astonished to find herself so light after nine months of fatigue duty.

And you go right along, lighter than nature, as if taking advantage of an intermission of lightness before another act begins, even making of this swing of deliverance a bait for future encumbrances! I call this all aberration, frivolity. Do you follow me?"

"Yes, yes, I hadn't thought of it all that way. But I shall observe myself carefully, and I will do everything according to your principles, my dear."

"No, there's no use thinking about it—it's something that is incurable. Come now, no more tears! Don't cry, please! You know that I can't stand tears."

Lohengrin delicately passes his hand over her throat to calm her.

"What remarkable hands you have," she says.

Elsa lies as still as death, remembering that this remarkable knight's first compliment was for her swanlike neck. But no, his hand pauses at one point . . .

"What's that called?"

"I don't know; the Adam's apple."

"Yes?"

"The Adam's apple."

"And that doesn't remind you of anything?"

"Heavens, no."

"Well, really . . . now. It reminds me of the worst days of our human history! Oh, don't cry. Don't cry! It's all over, I tell you I won't go on."

"You promise, dear?"

"Now let me doze off for a moment, let me commune with myself for a quarter of an hour in the silence of the night—and then, in the name of this delectable night, I give you my word that I shall set about adoring you as grandly as you deserve."

"As you wish, darling."

Lohengrin, that remarkable knight, turns his back to her. And then seizing hold of his pillow in a mad embrace, pressing it awkwardly against his chest and then against his cheek, he begins wailing into it like a child, a really incurable child.

"O lovely, lovely pillow, as soft and white as Elsa. Oh, my little Elsa, my innocent baby astonished at my profundity, my succulent, deliciously nubile baby, my lovely surprise packet, what a lucky find I have made in your divine body! Ah, I want to inch along in my love for you, I want to find the way to your heart! . . .

"Where are you? Where are you? How I love every bit of you! O lovely, lovely pillow, soon you won't have a single cool place for my forehead (after this exhausting day!). My lovely pillow, pure and white as a swan! Do you hear me?

"Do you hear me, my swan, my swan! May it always be you, pallid and mute forever—just you.

"I cling to your nonsinkable throat; carry me far across the immaculate seas; sweep me off, poor Ganymede, on your spiraling wings past the shores of the Milky Way, beyond the hailstorms of stars, around the deceptive cape of the Sun; fly back toward the Holy Grail where Parsifal, my father, is at work on a plan for the redemption of our little sister who is so human and so down-to-earth! . . .

"All this you know, my good, kind swan. I am waiting, I am still, I am holding my breath! Farewell! . . ."

Ah, then the window of the nuptial chamber burst wildly open with a cyclone of lunar enchantment. And the pillow, transformed into a swan, spread its imperial wings, and rose, bearing young Lohengrin on its back. It sailed in sidereal spirals off into the far-reaching expanse of thought, off over the desolate empty reaches of the sea, oh, far beyond the sea, toward the altitudes of Metaphysical Love, toward the glacial mirrors on which no young lady will ever breathe and trace with her finger on the frosted glass her name and the date.

And so it is that since then on such nights, in their cold and inviolable way, poets celebrate within their skulls a certain little Feast of the Assumption.

*Un melon mis à mûrir sur un
rebord de fenêtre de mansarde*
(A melon left to ripen on an
attic windowsill)

Unpublished drawing
From a notebook of 1884–85

Laforgue's notes for the Aquarium section of "Salome."
From a notebook of 1884–85

Laforgue's notes for the Aquarium section of "Salome."
From a notebook of 1884–85

Unpublished drawings
From a notebook of 1884–85

SALOME

Birth is going out; death is going back in.

    —Proverbs of the Kingdom of Annam,
    collected by Father Jourdain
    of the Foreign Missions

Two thousand dog-stars ago that very day a simple rhythmic revolution of the Palace Mandarins had placed the first Tetrarch, a lowly Roman proconsul, on the throne of the Esoteric White Islands, which have since been lost to history. The throne was made a carefully superintended inheritance that could henceforth keep this unique designation of Tetrarch—as inviolable in its sound as Monarch, and carrying in addition the many symbolisms of state attached to *tetra* in contrast to the single one carried by *monos*.

Built into three blocks with squat, unadorned pylons, internal courtyards, galleries, cellars, and the famous hanging gardens with their jungles growing lushly green in the Atlantic breezes, and the observatory with its watchtower poised two hundred meters up in the sky, and with its hundred ramps flanked by sphinxes and cynocephali, the Tetrarchic Palace was nothing but a monolith, which had been rough-hewn, excavated, scooped, and finally polished out of a mountain of white-veined black basalt. A final echoing strip of pavement, lined with rows of deep-mourning violet poplars in jars, projected into the touching solitude of the sea as far out as this eternal rock: the whole thing looked like a petrified sponge holding a pretty comic-opera lighthouse for the noctambulant junks.

Titanic, funereal, livid-streaked mass! How mystically these façades of black ivory reflect the day's July sun, the sun, which thus reflected in black on the sea, the owls of the hanging gardens can contemplate comfortably from atop the dusty pines.

At the end of the pier, the galley, which the evening before had brought these two intruding princes, the supposed son and nephew of a certain Satrap of the North, swung at its moorings, the subject of comment by a few silhouettes, lazy but restrained in their gestures, as is the native manner.

Now, since the festivities were not scheduled to burst forth officially until three o'clock, the palace slept heavily under the stagnant midday sun, and it was going to be late in dragging itself out of its siesta.

In the courtyard where the gutters converged, one could hear the attendants of the Princes of the North joking with the Tetrarch's household, roaring with laughter without understanding one another, playing quoits, exchanging tobacco. These foreign colleagues were being shown how white elephants are curried. . .

"But there are no white elephants where we come from," the Northerners observed.

And they watched the grooms cross themselves as if to ward off the effect of impious remarks. Later the foreigners stood gaping at the peacocks strutting around above the fountain, spreading their tails in the sunlight, and then enjoying, even unduly, the guttural echoes which, in the chaotic arrangement of all this layered rock, their barbaric cries provided.

The Tetrarch Emerald-Archetypas appeared on the central terrace, removing his gloves in the presence of that Epic Bard, the Universal Sun at its Zenith, Glow-worm of the Empyrean, etc., and the attendants hurried back inside to get on with their work. Now there he is, the Tetrarch, caryatid of dynasties, on the terrace!

Behind him lay the city, already loud with festivities, the streets slowly drying after a heavy sprinkling; and farther on, beyond the mock ramparts all dotted with yellow flowerets, how happily the plain stretched out in the distance: pretty roads with little heaps of crushed flint and a checkerboard of variegated fields. Before him, the sea, always new and respectable—yes, since there is no other name for it—the Sea.

And the only punctuation of the silence was now the joyful clear barking of dogs, which urchins, shiningly naked among the mica of the burning sands, with their exotic whistling, sent running against the oncoming breakers, breakers along which these children had just been skipping their discarded arrowheads.

Leaning now on one elbow in the coolness of the invisible streams, among the clematis of the terrace, the Tetrarch was sulkily exhaling the smoke of his midday hookah in desultory, sad, and artless meanderings. Yesterday, for a moment, on the suspect arrival of a messenger announcing these Princes of the North, his destiny, already so fortunate on these fortunate islands, had wavered between immediate domestic terror and an absolute dilettantism that enjoys staking its all on a debacle.

For the prisoner who was now meditating on his fate deep in the only dungeon of the Tetrarchic Palace was himself one of these sons of the North, one of these meat-eaters, with hairy faces. The unfortunate Iaokanann had ended up here one fine morning with his spectacles and his unkempt red beard, holding forth in the language of the country about the pamphlets which he distributed free of charge, but boosting them in such aggressive fashion that the people had been on the point of stoning him.

After so many esoteric and uneventful centuries, was the twentieth centenary of the Emerald-Archetypas dynasty to be celebrated by the fireworks of a war with the other world? Iaokanann had spoken of his own country as a land dwarfed by poverty, hungry for the possessions of others, cultivating war as a national industry. And these two princes might well be coming to claim this individual, who was certainly a man of genius after all and one of their subjects and they might well be planning to complicate the pretext and exhibit one of those rights of Western peoples. . .

How fortunate then—thanks to the inexplicable intercessions of his daughter Salome—that he had not disturbed the executioner's traditional and purely honorary sinecure by sending him to Iaokanann with the sacred Kris.

But what a false alarm it had been! The two princes were simply making a voyage around the world searching for vaguely occupied colonies, and had merely put in at the White Islands in passing, out of curiosity. Well, of all things, so it was in this outpost that their old scoundrel Iaokanann was to end up by getting himself hanged? They had been avid to know every detail of the tribulations of the poor devil who had proved to be so little of a prophet in his own country.

So the Tetrarch was nursing his midday hookah in a vacant manner, his temper as shattered as it usually was at this culminating hour—more shattered even today with the mounting noises of national festivities, firecrackers, and bands, with all the bunting and soft drinks.

Tomorrow morning the galley bearing these gentlemen would slip over the seemingly infinite horizon beyond which various other nations were said to live under the same hot sun.

Then, leaning over the tile balustrade through the syrupy clematis and crumbling brioches for the fish in the ponds on the lower terraces, Emerald-Archetypas was congratulating himself on no longer having to subsist even on the small return from his failing faculties, since his venerable carcass decidedly discouraged all the galvanisms of art, meditation, of kindred spirits, and industry.

And to think that on the day of his birth a remarkable storm had broken over the black dynastic palace, and that several reliable witnesses had seen a flash of lightning spell out the words *alpha* and *omega!* How many high noons had been lost sighing over that mystical hocus-pocus. Nothing special had manifested itself. But then, after all, *alpha* and *omega* are open to many interpretations.

In the end, not quite two months ago, having decided that he was no longer young, and making desperate efforts to revive a bit of the enthusiastic acceptance of the void that had made his twentieth year so ascetic, he had begun a regimen of daily pilgrimages through the necropolis, which, besides holding the bones of his ancestors, was so delightfully cool in the summer. . . Winter would be coming on with the ceremonies of the Snow Cult and the investiture of his grandson. And then he still had Salome, that dear child, who refused to hear of the joys of marriage.

Emerald-Archetypas was just striking a bell to call for more of the brioches consecrated to the deluxe July fish when on the tile behind him resounded the bronze cane of the Ordainer-of-the-Thousand-Odds-and-Ends. The Princes of the North had returned from their visit to the city; they were awaiting the Tetrarch in the Hall of the Mandarins.

—— II ——

The aforementioned Princes of the North, girded, pomaded, gloved, and uniformed, with full-flowing beards and parted hair (with locks curved down around their temples to give tone to the profiles stamped on their medallions), were waiting, one hand holding the helmet on the right hip while the other—with the prancing gesture of a stallion catching a whiff of gunpowder—fidgeted with the saber on the left one. They were conversing with the court officials: the Great Mandarin, the Lord Master of the Libraries, the Arbiter of Elegance, the Keeper of Symbols, the Tutor of Selection and of the Gynaeceum, the Pope of the Snow Cult, and the Administrator of Death, between two lines of thin, swift scribes, who had their quill pens hanging at their sides and their inkwells slung over their hearts.

Their Highnesses congratulated the Tetrarch, felicitating themselves on the happy wind that . . . on such a glorious day . . . on these islands—and they ended with a eulogy of the capital, in which the White Basilica, where they had heard a *Te deum lauda-mus* played on the barrel organ of Seven Sorrows, and the Burial Ground of Beasts and Things were not the least among the curiosities.

A light meal was brought in. And since the Princes had scruples about touching meat among hosts so orthodoxly vegetarian and ichthyophagous, the table was a lovely still-life, with its delicate arrangement of callipygian artichokes swimming among the crystal in bristling wrought-iron, hinged shells, asparagus on trays of pink rushes, pearl-gray eels, date cakes, and an endless array of compotes and sweet wines.

After the collation, preceded by the Ordainer-of-the-Thousand-Odds-and-Ends, the Tetrarch and his attendants took it upon themselves to show the Palace, the titanic, funereal, white-veined Palace, to their guests.

They would go up first to enjoy the panoramic view of the islands from the observatory, and then descend, level by level, through the park, the Menageries, and the Aquarium, to the cellars below.

Hoisted up—and pneumatically, at that—to the top, the procession tiptoed briskly through the apartments of Salome, whence, with much slamming of doors, two or three Negresses withdrew their oily bronze shoulder blades. In the very center of the room, tiled with majolica (oh, what yellow majolica), they saw an enormous ivory basin that had been abandoned with quite a large white sponge, some satin things left to soak, and a pair of pink (oh, what pink) sandals. After a booklined room, and then another filled with metallic therapeutic apparatus, they reached a circular staircase, and breathed in the elevated air of a terrace— and all just in time to see a young lady melodiously cobwebbed in jonquil chiffon with black polka dots glide down through space, on a series of pulleys, toward other levels of the castle.

The Princes, who had already been thrown into a confusion of salaams by their intrusion, were suddenly speechless before a circle of astonished eyes that seemed to confess with embarrassment, "It's really quite all right, you know; nothing here concerns us."

And then uttering breathless little words of admiration, they began circulating around the dome of the observatory housing a grand equatorial eighteen meters wide, a mobile dome decorated with waterproof frescoes and whose mass of one hundred thousand kilograms floating on fourteen steel girders in a bath of magnesium chloride could spin around in two minutes at the touch, it seemed, of Salome's hand.

What if these ridiculously exotic characters suddenly took it into their heads to throw us overboard, the two Princes thought as they both shuddered. But, after all, they were ten times more robust, those two in their tight uniforms, than the ten or twelve pale, hairless characters, their fingers covered with rings, sacerdotally entangled in their coruscating gold lamé. And so they contented themselves with spotting their galley below in the harbor, shining like a beetle with its armor of polished steel.

And they listened to the enumeration of these islands, an archipelago of variegated flora and fauna.

They went back down through a Hall of Perfumes where the Arbiter of Elegance pointed out, among the gifts their Highnesses would be good enough to take with them, all products of Salome's occult compounding: rouges made without carbonate of lead, powders made without white lead or bismuth, aphrodisiacs without Spanish fly, bath salts without protochloride of mercury, depilatories without sulphurate of arsenic, milks without corrosive sublimate or oxide of hydrated lead, true vegetable dyes without silver nitrate, hyposulphate of soda, copper sulphate, cyanide of potassium, lead acetate (is that possible!), and two demijohns of distilled spring and autumn essences.

At the end of a hot, damp, interminable corridor, having a look of ambush about it, the Ordainer opened a door green with moss and fungi worthy of jewel boxes, and they found themselves amid the great silence of the famous hanging gardens—ah, just in time to watch, rustling around a bend, a young form hermetically cobwebbed in jonquil chiffon with black polka dots, escorted by mastiffs and greyhounds, whose frisking barks, sobbing with fidelity, drifted off to be lost in distant echoes.

Oh, it was all filled with the echoes of unknown corridors, this kilometrically deep solitude of severe green, watered with streaks of light, holding nothing but an army of straight pine trees, with bare trunks of a salmony flesh tint, opening up high, very high, their dusty parasols. The bars of the sun's rays rested between these trunks with the same sweetness that they would on the pillars of some claustral chapel with grilled windows. A sea breeze had just blown through this lofty forest like the strange distant noise of a freight train in the night. Then the silence of great altitudes, completely in its element, returned. Somewhere very near a bulbul could be heard disgorging its distinguished garrulities; somewhere far off, another bulbul answered it, as if they, too, felt completely in their element, in their age-old dynastic aviary. The Princes moved on, feeling the thickness of this artificial soil, which, padded with dead leaves and the layered pine needles of a thousand yesterdays, so easily held the roots of these patriarchal pines. Then on past great abysses of greensward, green slopes calling forth dreams of dancing fauns, on past stagnant lakes where swans, wearing earrings much too heavy for their slender throats, were sinking with age and boredom, past hundreds of decamerons of polychrome statues, which had broken off from their pedestals into poses of a surprising . . . nobility.

Finally the deer park, with its gazelles but with no other pretensions, made the transition between the orchards and the Menagerie and Aquarium.

The beasts did not deign to lift their eyelids: the elephants swayed, rustling their rough, crimped coats, but with their thoughts elsewhere; the giraffes, despite their soft café-au-lait clothing, seemed a bit overbearing in their insistence on gazing far above these dazzling courtiers; the monkeys did not for a minute interrupt the intimate scenes of their phalanstery; the aviaries scintillated deafeningly; the snakes went right on changing their skins, as they had for over a week; the stables had just been stripped of their most handsome stallions, mares, and zebras, which had been lent to the municipality for the day's cavalcade.

The Aquarium! Ah, indeed, the Aquarium! Let us pause here. How it revolves in silence!

A labyrinth of grottoes arranged in corridors to the right and left with luminous glassed-in vistas of submarine countries. Moors with dolmens incrusted with viscous gems, tiered arenas of basalt, where pairs of crabs with an obtuse and fumbling good after-dinner humor and little jovial dead-pan eyes become entangled. . .

Plains of sand so fine that it is frequently blown about by wind from the tail of a flatfish arriving from afar with the soft undulations of an oriflamme of liberty, and which is inspected, as it goes by, goes on, and leaves us behind, by half-buried pop-eyes which it serves as the only reading matter.

And the desolation of steppes occupied by a single blasted, ossified tree, its branches colonized by clusters of quivering hippocampi.

And, under the enjambments of natural bridges, long mossy ravines in which ruminate in the mire the slate-covered carapaces of rat-tailed king crabs, some seeming to writhe upside down but probably just doing it on purpose to give themselves a rubdown.

And beneath chaotic ruined triumphal arches, eels drifting about like frivolous ribbons; and random migrations of hirsute nuclei, tufted eyelashes surrounding a matrix that uses them to fan itself during the tedium of long journeys.

And fields of sponges like a wreckage of lungs; truffles in orange velvet; a whole cemetery of pearly molluscs; and asparagus beds preserved in the alcohol of Silence. . .

As far as the eye can see, meadows enameled with white sea anemones, fat ripe onions, bulbs with violet membranes, bits of tripe straying here and there and seeming to make a new life for itself, stumps with antennae winking at the neighboring coral, a thousand aimless warts; a whole fetal, claustral, vibrating flora, trembling with the eternal dream of one day being able in whispers to congratulate itself on this state of things. . .

Ah, then, perched on a high plateau, glued like a leech, the lookout octopus, fat, hairless minotaur of an entire region. . .

The procession pauses, and, before leaving, the Pope of the Snow Cult addresses it as if reciting some ancient lesson:

"Here no day, no night, Gentlemen, no winter, no spring, no summer, no autumn, no other chopping and changing of weather. Loving, dreaming, without moving, in the cool of imperturbable blindness. O satisfied world, you dwell in a blind and silent blessedness, while we dry up with our superterrestrial pangs of hunger. Why aren't the antennae of our own senses bounded by Blindness, Opacity, and Silence? Why must they seek out what is beyond their proper domain? Why can't we curl up, encrusted in our little corners, to sleep off the drunken deaths of our own little Egos?

"And yet, O submarine watering-places, our superterrestrial hungers afford us two pleasures of your type: one, the face of the dearly beloved asleep on the pillow beside us, with her damp bands of hair and a wounded mouth with white teeth lighted by one of the Moon's aquarium rays.—(Oh, do not touch, do not touch!)—the other, the Moon itself, that flat, yellow, revolving sunflower dried out by agnosticism. (Oh, try to touch it if you can!)"

So that was the Aquarium; but did these foreign Princes understand anything at all about it?

And they filed quickly and discreetly down the central corridor of the Gynaeceum, painted with eugenic scenes, its melancholy atmosphere pervaded by feminine aromatics; and all they could hear—to the right and to the left—was the splashing of a cool fountain, wetting the thread of an unforgettably captive, unfortunate, and sterile song.

And since their ignorance of the local rites might lead them to commit some fatal blunder, the Princes crossed with the same discreet step the Tetrarchic necropolis, consisting of two rows of wall cupboards hidden behind full-length portraits and containing vials and hundreds of realistic relics—things that had sentimental attraction only for the family, which is quite understandable.

But what they really wanted to see was their old friend Iaokanann!

So they followed a functionary with a key embroidered across his spine. He stopped at the end of a trench smelling of niter and pointed out a grill, which he had lowered breast-high so they might look into the cell of this unfortunate European as he rose from the floor, where he had been lying, face buried in a heap of wretched papers.

Hearing himself greeted cordially in his native tongue, Iaokanann had stood up and adjusted his huge spectacles that had been patched with string.

Oh, my God, to have his Princes here! On many a nasty winter evening, his wooden shoes soggy with filthy snow, in the front rank of the poor devils going home from their day of paid labor, and, for a moment held in line by tyrannical mounted policemen, he had stood and watched them descend in their plumed hats from their state carriages, and, between two rows of officers presenting arms, climb the grand stairway of the palace, the palace at whose *a giorno* windows he would shake his fist, murmuring each time that "the time is drawing near!" And evidently the time had come, and the promised revolution had taken place, and God had called upon his old prophet Iaokanann; and now this royal intervention on his behalf, this lengthy heroic expedition of his Princes come to deliver him—their visit was no doubt the touching consecration the people had demanded, stamping him irrevocably as the agent of a Universal Resurrection!

He bowed automatically from the waist, in the fashion of his country, while searching about for a memorable phrase, something fraternal, but also worthy. . .

His search was abruptly cut off by the nephew of the Satrap of the North, that bald apoplectic old trooper who scoffed at everyone for no reason, and following the lead of Napoleon I, cursed all "visionaries": "Aha, there you are, visionary, scribbler, reformed convict, bastard son of Jean-Jacques Rousseau. So this is where you've come to get yourself hanged, outcast hack! Good riddance! May your filthy top-knot soon drop into the guillotine basket along with the other heads that hatched the Conspiracy of the Lower Wood. Yes, the heads that dropped recently from the foul Conspiracy of the Lower Wood."

Oh, brutes, ineradicable brutes! So the Conspiracy of the Lower Wood had failed! His brethren had been assassinated, and no one would give him the human details. It was all over, over; and there was nothing to do but be crushed under the Authoritarian heel. The unfortunate publicist turned resolutely toward silence, waiting for all these fashionable people to retire and leave him to die in his little corner; two long white tears streamed under his spectacles and down his emaciated cheeks toward his threadbare beard. And suddenly they saw him rise up on his bare feet and hold out his hands toward an apparition to which he sobbed out the tenderest diminutives of his native tongue. The Princes turned around—ah, just in time to hear a rattling of keys in the twilight of this *in pace,* and to watch a disappearing form completely cobwebbed in jonquil chiffon covered with black polka dots. . . .

And Iaokanann fell back face down on his mattress, and, seeing that he had just turned over the inkwell on his stack of papers, he began to dry up the ink with a childlike tenderness.

Without any comment, the procession went back up the stairs, while the nephew of the Satrap of the North, toying with his rigid high collar, mulled over a few principles.

—— III ——

In an allegro and fatalistic mode, an orchestra of ivory instruments was improvising a unanimous little overture.

The court entered, greeted by the rich stir of two hundred

luxurious guests rising from their handsome couches. It paused a moment before a pyramid of gifts that had been offered to the Tetrarch during the day. The two Princes of the North nudged one another, each urging his companion to remove the Order of the Iron Fleece from his throat to put it on that of his host. Neither one dared to do so. It was obvious, especially in these surroundings, that this collar had no artistic worth. And as for its honorary worth, since they saw nothing of this kind around them, they felt that the explanations needed to point up the value of their gift would either fall flat or meet with only limited acceptance.

The court installed itself; Emerald-Archetypas presented his son and his grandson, both superb products (superb in the Esoteric and White sense, naturally) and emblematically embellished.

Then, from the center of this airy hall strewn with jonquil rushes, lined with deafening aviaries, a fountain pierced a striped white-rubber velarium, and fell back on it in a cold and crackling rain; below, along the semicircular tables were ten rows of couches, each adorned according to the special qualifications of the guest occupying it. Facing them was a marvelously deep stage set representing a garden of the Alcazar, before which the flower of the Islands' mountebanks, jugglers, beauties, and virtuosos were to shed their varied talents.

A sly breeze ran the length of the velarium, which was already weighed down by the incessant downpour of the fountain.

And the aviaries, happy with their clashing of colors, quieted down regretfully when the musical accompaniment to the meal began.

Poor Tetrarch! All this music, this parterre of luxurious respect, this whole pompous day annoyed him no end. He hardly touched the ingenious succession of dishes, pecking at them with the snow-capped spatulas of his teeth, forgetting himself like a child, gaping at the circus-frieze that now unfolded before the Alcazar.

There, on the stage, were:

The serpent-girl, slender, and viscously scaled in blue, green, and yellow, her throat and body a touching pink: she flowed and turned, insatiably in contact with herself, all the while lisping the hymn beginning: "Byblis, my sister Byblis, you have changed into a spring! . . ."

Then a procession of thoroughly novel sacramental costumes, each symbolizing a human desire. What affectation!

Then interludes of level cyclones of electrified flowers, a whirlwind of bouquets absolutely beside themselves! . . .

Then the musical clowns, each wearing over his heart the cranks of real barrel organs that they kept turning in the manner of Messiahs who will not be pushed from their path but who will carry on to the very limit of their apostolate.

Three other clowns impersonated the Idea, the Will, and the Unconscious. Idea chattered on about everything under the sun, Will butted his head against the scenery, and Unconscious made the grand mysterious gestures of one who knows basically much more than he can express. Moreover, this trinity had one identical refrain:

> O Canaan
> Of the Vacuum!
> O Vacuum, Delphi
> Of the Library!

It was a hilarious success.

Then some virtuosos of the flying trapeze, with almost sidereal ellipses!

Attendants then brought in a platform of real ice: a teenage skater sprang forth upon it, arms crossed over the white astrakhan frogging on his chest, and he did not stop until he had executed all known combinations of curves. He waltzed on his toes like a ballerina; etched on the ice a flamboyant Gothic cathedral, without omitting a single rose window or delicate carved detail; danced a three-part fugue, ending in a whirlwind as inextricable as that of a fakir possessed *del diavolo*, and then left the stage, feet in the air, skating off on fingernails of steel. . .

The performance was brought to a close by a procession of living tableaux—of nudes as modest as plants, gradually transformed, through aesthetic tribulation, into eurhythmic symbols.

Hookahs had been handed round; conversation had become general; Iaokanann, who was surely not cheered up by the sound of these festivities above his head, bore the brunt of it all. The Princes of the North spoke of armed authority as the supreme religion, the sentinel of peace, the guarantor of daily bread and of international understanding. They got all mixed up in what they were saying, and to come to the point, recited, as epiphenomenon, this couplet:

> Every honest man believes
> In the evolution of his Species.

The Mandarins countered that it was better to withdraw into oneself, to neutralize the sources of social competition, and to shut oneself up in segregated coteries of initiates living sparely and peacefully within great walls, etc., etc.

And the music, playing on, seemed to continue with what they were too ephemeral to formulate.

Finally fell a silence that enlarged like a pale-meshed net thrown in the evening on the water by fishermen expecting a fine catch; they all got up—it seems it was Salome.

She came down the circular staircase, erect in her chiffon sheath; with one hand she waved the guests back to their couches; a little black lyre hung from her wrist; with her fingertips she threw a kiss to her father.

She went to stand on the stage, in front of the drawn Alcazar curtain, waiting for everyone to feast his eyes on her to the full, amusing herself by putting on a bold front and swaying on her blood-drained feet, her toes spread apart.

She paid attention to no one. Dusted with unidentified pollen,

her hair hung down over her shoulders, tousled on her forehead
with yellow flowers and twisted blades of straw. Below her naked
shoulders and held by mother-of-pearl straps hung the fan of a
dwarf peacock, with its changing tones of moiré, azure, gold, emerald, the whole a halo on which rose her candid head with the
superior but cordial carelessness of feeling itself unique, her neck
bent as if severed, and her eyes distorted by iridescent expiations,
her mouth revealing, under the pale pink circumflex accent of her
lips, teeth set in a paler pink, bared in a most crucified smile.

Oh, the gentle celestial creature whose aesthetics are so well
known, the exquisite recluse of the Esoteric White Islands! . . .

She was hermetically cobwebbed in jonquil chiffon with black
polka dots, and the cobweb, caught up by clasps here and there,
leaving her arms in their angelic nudity, fell as a sash between the
two faint suspicions of breasts with the nipples tipped with carnations—a sash given her on her eighteenth birthday, embroidered
and hooked on a little higher than her lovely umbilical dimple to
a ruffled girdle of an intense and jealous yellow. It then settled,
an inviolable pelvic shadow in the grasp of her narrow hips, fell
to her ankles, and finally went back up behind in two separate
floating folds which were attached to the rear of the mother-of-
pearl straps holding the fan of the dwarf peacock with its shifting
colors: blue, moiré, emerald, gold—a halo for her candid and superior head. She stood there swaying on her bloodless feet with
her toes spread apart, feet shod only in anklets of gold from which
fell dazzling fringes of yellow watered silk.

Oh, the little womb-endowed Messiah! How heavy was her
head! She didn't know what to do with her hands, and even her
shoulders bothered her a bit. Who could have crucified the smile
of this little Immaculate Conception? And distorted the blue of
her gaze? Oh, all hearts rejoiced in how simple her skirt must feel!
How long art is, and how short is life! If one could but converse
with her in some little corner near a fountain, not to discover her
wherefore but rather her how, and then to die! . . . to die unless. . .

Perhaps she will tell us something after all?

Leaning slightly forward amid the silky sunken cushions, the wrinkles of his face dilated, the pupils of his eyes spurting forth from behind the battlements of their ungilded lids, toying nervously with the Seal that hung from his neck, the Tetrarch had just given a page, along with his turreted tiara, the pineapple on which he had been chewing.

"Collect your thoughts, collect your thoughts, before you begin, O Idea and Elegance, Caryatid of these trouble-free Islands," he implored.

Then he smiled at the whole room, with the air of a proud father, as if to say, "You will see what you will see," in a somewhat confused fashion, giving his princely guests to understand that to provide for the little person in question the Moon had bled itself white, and that she was generally conceded to be (there had been a Council on the subject) the foster sister of the Milky Way (nothing was too good for her!).

Now with her hip raised and her weight resting delicately on her right foot, her other leg bent back like one of Niobe's daughters, Salome, having let out a little coughing laugh, perhaps just to let the audience know that she didn't take herself seriously, drew blood from her black lyre, and with the toneless and sexless voice of a patient calling for medicine he needs no more than you or I, began to improvise:

"How estimable the Void is! The Void, that is to say, the Latent Life that will flower the day after tomorrow at the earliest—how estimable, how absolving, co-existing with Infinity, just as limpid as it can be!"

Was she joking? She continued:

"Love, inclusive mania of not wanting to die absolutely, shabby loophole, false brother that you are, I shall not tell you that it is high time you explain yourself. In eternity things are as they are. But in the name of the Unconscious, it would be good to make some mutual concessions in the domain of the five present senses!

"O latitudes, altitudes, from the nebulae of Good Will to the little medusas of fresh water, do me the favor of going to graze in the empirical orchards. O Passengers of this Earth, which is eminently similar to incalculable others just as alone in infinity with their indefinite work. The active essential loves itself—now follow me carefully—loves itself dynamically, more or less according to its own inclination: it's a lovely soul that plays indefinitely on its own bagpipe—let it play. Now, all of you, be naturally passive: as automatic as Everything, enter into the Orders of Well-intentioned Harmony. And let me know how you make out.

"Yes, hydrocephalic theosophists and gentle-winged representatives of the populace, all ordinary groups of phenomena without guarantee from the government of the beyond, return to your natural state of carelessness, day after day, season after season, graze upon these sphinxless deltas, the sum of whose angles is still equal to two right angles. That is the most fitting behavior, you incurably pubescent generations; and especially feign entanglement in the irresponsible limbo of the virtualities of which I have spoken. The Unconscious *farà da se.*

"And you, fatal Jordans, Baptismal Ganges, insubmersible sidereal currents, all maternal cosmogonies! Before you enter, wash yourself clean of the more or less original stain of the Systematic so that we may be chewed to bits in advance for the Great Curative (or one might say, Palliative) Virtue that patches up meadows and epidermises alike, etc. . . *Quia est in ea virtus dormitiva* . . . So . . ."

Salome stopped short, threw back her hair powdered with unidentified pollen, her slight breasts panting so furiously that the carnations fell from them, baring the widowed nipples. To recover, she drew from her black lyre an irrelevant fugue. . .

"Oh, go on, go on, tell us everything you know!" whimpered Emerald-Archetypas, clapping his hands like a child. "Upon my Tetrarchic word, you shall have anything you want—the University, my Seal, the Snow Cult. Inoculate us with the grace of your

Immaculate Conception. . . I am bored, we are all so thoroughly bored, are we not, Gentlemen?"

The auditors exhaled a real noise of unprecedented discomfort; tiaras were nodding. They were ashamed of one another, but the human heart being weak, even in so well-bred a race . . . (You understand me, my good neighbor.)

After a brief survey of theogonies, theodicies, and formulae for behavior regarding free will in various countries (all with the abruptness of a choirmaster who says, "One measure for good measure, all right?"), Salome continued her mystical garrulity, a bit frantic, her face convulsed, her Adam's apple throbbing frightfully—as if she herself might soon be no more than a cobweb sheath through which would shine a soul like a droplet from a meteor.

O tides, lunar oboes, avenues, twilit lawns, shoddy November winds, hay-gathering, vocations missed, animal glances, vicissitudes! Jonquil chiffon with funereal polka dots, distracted eyes, crucified smiles, adorable navels, peacock aureoles, fallen carnations, irrelevant fugues! They could feel themselves being reborn, raw, fresh from the beyond, with their systematic souls exhaling themselves in spirals across downpours with indubitably definitive noises for the good of the Earth, and understood by everything, endowed by Varuna, the Universal Air, which made sure that one was ready.

And Salome was wildly emphatic:

"This is the pure state, I tell you! O Sectarians of consciousness, why label yourselves individuals—indivisible, that is to say? Blow upon the thistle down of these sciences during the rise of my northern constellations!

"Are you really living when you insist on understanding yourself along with everything else? When you stop at every stage and ask yourself: 'Ah, who is fooling whom now?'

"Away with cadres, species, kingdoms. Nothing is lost, nothing is added, everything is everyone's; the Prodigal Son is tamed in advance, and with no need to confess (his downfall will come as it must, at the slightest hint).

"These are not pretexts for expiations and new downfalls; they are vintages trampled out by the Infinite, not experimental, but fatal, because. . .

"You are the other sex, and we are the little feminine playmates of your childhood (although always, of course, as elusive Psyches). Starting this very evening, let us plunge into the harmonious goodness of heart of pre-established moralities; let the current sweep us along, our flowering bellies open to the air, amid the aromas of necessary waste and slaughter, toward the great beyond where we will no longer feel the beating of our hearts or the pulse of our consciousness.

"We advance in a dance, to cadenzas of stanzas, the salves of valves, lewd causes without pauses; in bleached surplices let us abdicate toward the obliquity of the primitive pull of the current, all well beyond the Ego! (Not sure that I'm with it.)"

The little yellow wailing woman with the funereal polka dots broke her lyre across her knee and regained her dignity.

The intoxicated auditors, to cover their embarrassment, wiped their brows; a silence of inexpressible confusion swept over them.

The Princes of the North dared not take out their watches, much less ask, "When is her bedtime?" It could hardly be later than six o'clock.

The Tetrarch scrutinized the designs on his cushions; it was all over; Salome's harsh voice made him sit up abruptly:

"And now, father, I should like you to send Iaokanann's head up to me. Have it put on some kind of platter. I have spoken. I shall go up and wait for it."

"But surely, child, you can't mean what you say! That poor foreigner . . ."

But the entire hall, by a nodding of tiaras, gave its fervent approval that this day the will of Salome should be done; and the aviaries finished it off by resuming their deafening scintillations.

Emerald-Archetypas let one eye drift toward the Princes of the North; not the least sign of approval or disapproval. Evidently this was no concern of theirs.

Adjudicated!

The Tetrarch threw his Seal to the Administrator of Death.

The diners were already beginning to disperse, chatting of other things, in the direction of their evening baths.

—— IV ——

Leaning from the parapet of the observatory, Salome, turning from the national festivities, listened to the sea make the familiar sounds it makes on beautiful evenings.

One of those complete star-filled nights! Eternities of embers at the zenith! What a night replete with reasons for hopping an express train and riding off into exile!

Salome, foster sister of the Milky Way, hardly ever became her full self except when the stars appeared.

Following a color photograph (thanks to spectrum analysis) of the so-called yellow, red, and white stars of the sixteenth magnitude, she had had diamonds cut to proportionate sizes to strew over her hair and over her entire beauty and over her night dress (mourning-violet chiffon with golden polka dots) when she went out on the terraces to confer intimately with her twenty-four million stars, just as a sovereign, when receiving his peers or satellites, puts on the decorations of their various regions.

Salome had only contempt for the vulgar cabochons of the first and second magnitude. Stars below the fifteenth magnitude did not belong to her world. But the nebular matrices were really her passion; not the nebulae fully formed with planetary discs, but the formless, the perforated, the tentacled ones. And Orion, that gaseous blot with its ailing rays, remained the uncontested favorite among the jewels of her twinkling crown.

Ah, dear companions of stellar meadows, Salome was no longer

just little Salome—tonight she planned to launch a new era in relations and etiquette!

In the first place, exorcised of the virginity of her tissue, she
felt now, in relation to these nebulous matrices, fecundated like
them by gyratory evolutions.

Then, too, this fatal sacrifice to the cult (still she was lucky to
get out of it so cheaply!) had obliged her to pay her initiation fee
in the form of an act—a serious one, whatever you say—named
homicide.

Finally, to insure the deathly silence of the Initiator, she had
to serve these contingent people, although cut with water, the
elixir distilled from the anxiety of a hundred nights of this caliber.

Well, it was her life; and she was a speciality, a little speciality.

There, then, on a cushion amid the wreckage of the ebony lyre,
shone the head of John (like the head of Orpheus of old) coated
with phosphor, washed, rouged, curled, grinning at these twenty-
four million stars.

As soon as the object had been delivered, Salome, to appease
her scientific conscience, had tried the famous, much-discussed
postdecapitation experiments; as she had expected, her electric
caresses drew from the face nothing but inconsequential grimaces.

Now she knew what she was about.

But to think that she no longer lowered her eyes in the presence
of Orion! She stood erect and fixed her gaze for ten whole minutes on the mystic nebula of her puberty. How many nights, how
many future nights, would belong to the one who had the last
word.

And those bands, those firecrackers, down there in the city!

Salome finally shook herself like a reasonable person and raised
her sash; then lifting from her body the cloudy gold and gray
opal of Orion, she placed it like a sacramental wafer in John's
mouth, then kissed the mouth mercifully and hermetically, and
sealed it with her corrosive seal (all in a matter of minutes).

She waited a moment. No sign came from the night! . . . Then with an impatient and irritated "Come, now!" she grasped that inspired noddle in her delicate womanly hands. . .

Since she wanted the head to fall straight into the sea without being smashed to pieces on the rocks of the foundation, she took a run with it. The relic described a satisfactory phosphorescent parabola. Oh, a noble parabola! But the unlucky little astronomer had badly calculated her swing, and falling herself over the parapet, with at last a human cry, she toppled from rock to rock, with a death rattle at her throat, coming finally to rest in a deep picturesque hollow washed by the waves, far from the noises of national festivities, lacerated to the bone, her sidereal diamonds cutting into her flesh, her skull battered in, paralyzed by vertigo, in rather bad shape, at the point of death for a full hour.

And she did not even receive the last sacrament of seeing the phosphorescent star of John's head floating on the sea. . .

As for the distant heavens, they were distant.

So that was how Salome met her death—Salome of the White Esoteric Islands, that is; less a victim of illiterate chance than of the desire to live in a world of artifice and not in a simple, wholesome one like the rest of us.

PERSEUS AND ANDROMEDA
or the Happiest of the Three

— I —

Monotonous, unmerited Homeland! A lonely island, all gray and yellow dunes, lying under migratory skies; and everywhere the sea, limiting the view, stifling cries, hope and melancholy.

The Sea! No matter where viewed and no matter for how long, it is always the same whenever one comes on it—always itself, never at fault, always alone, an empire of unsociability, a great history remaining forever silent, a poorly directed cataclysm; as if the liquid state in which we see it is but the degeneration from some other state. And the days when it begins to set that liquid state in motion! And those more intolerable ones when it takes on the colors of a wound that has no surface to reflect itself in, and no one to staunch it! The Sea, always the indefatigable sea! In short, not the stuff of which lovers are made. (And to think that one must renounce such a notion, and even renounce the hope of sharing its rancors after the confidences one has had, no matter how long one has spent alone in its company.)

Monotonous and unmerited Homeland! When will all this end? And, as for the infinite: space monopolized by the more or less unlimited sea, time expressed solely by the heavens that are crossed by indifferent seasons with migrations of gray birds, complaining, untamable. What do we know about all this, what can we do about all this confused and ineffable sulking? If you were born with feeling, you were better off dead.

On this particular afternoon the sea is a nondescript dark green as far as the eye can see; and as far as the eye can see, a frothing of innumerable whitecaps lighting and relighting themselves, like a flock of innumerable sheep that swim, and sink, and reappear, sheep that never arrive, and finally will be overtaken by darkness. And above them out there the four winds, with their gamboling for art's sake, for the delight of killing the afternoon by whipping the foaming crests into rainbow spray. When a ray of sunlight passes it caresses the backs of the waves with a rainbow like a rich dolphin risen for a moment and then submerged, stupidly defiant.

And that is all. Unmerited and monotonous Homeland! . . .

Up to the very entrance of a little bay with two grottoes cushioned with eiderdown and pale beds of seaweed, the vast and monotonous sea gushes, gasping, against the island. But the sea's plaint does not drown out the shrill, harsh little moans of Andromeda, as she lies there stretched out on her stomach. Leaning on one elbow facing the horizon, she is observing, without thinking, the mechanism of the waves that go on dying and being reborn as far as the eye can see. Andromeda is moaning softly to herself. She moans; but suddenly she notices that her moans blend with those of the sea and the wind, two unsociable entities, two powerful parties that pay no attention whatever to her. She stops abruptly; then looks around her for something else to cling to.

"Monster!" she calls out.

"Child?"

"Eh, Monster!"

"Yes, child."

"What are you doing down there all this time?"

The Monster-Dragon, crouching at the entrance to his grotto, with his tail half in the water, turns around, his spine sparkling with all the riches of submarine Golcondas, lifts compassionately his eyelids fringed with many-colored cartilaginous passementeries, displays two large glaucous, watery eyes, and, with the voice of a distinguished man who has known sorrow, speaks:

"Can't you see, child, I am breaking up pebbles and polishing them for your slingshot; there'll be other flocks of birds flying by before sunset."

"Stop it; I can't stand that noise. And besides, I don't want to kill any more birds. Let them fly on back to their own countries. Oh, migratory birds that pass without seeing me, oh, hordes of waves coming here to die without bringing me anything. I can't tell you how bored I am! This time I'm really ill . . . Monster?"

"Yes, child."

"Tell me, why don't you bring me any more pretty stones? What have I done, uncle, to displease you?"

The Monster shrugs his shoulders sumptuously, scratches the sand on his right, picks up a pebble and takes a handful of pink pearls and crystallized anemones that he had been holding in reserve for just such an occasion, and lays them under Andromeda's pretty nose. Andromeda, still lying stretched out on the sand, sighs without moving:

"And suppose I refuse them with coldness, with inexplicable coldness?"

The Monster takes back his treasure, and sends it down into the darkness of its native submarine Golconda.

Then Andromeda rolls in the sand, and sighs, tossing her hair over her face in pitiful disorder:

"My rose-colored pearls, my crystallized anemones! This is too much, I shall die of it. And it will be your fault. Ah, you don't realize what a terrible wrong you have done!"

But she soon calms down, and runs, with her usual coquetry, to stretch out under the Monster's chin, throwing her white arms around his viscous purple neck. The Monster sumptuously shrugs his shoulders and begins to secrete a wild musk wherever he feels her little arms, those arms of the dear little child, who sighs:

"Oh, Monster, oh, Dragon, you tell me that you love me but cannot do anything for me. You see that I am being bored to death, and still you can't do anything for me. If you could do something and cure me, how I would love you!"

"Noble Andromeda, daughter of the King of Ethiopia! This Dragon, who is a Dragon in spite of himself, this poor Monster can only answer you by means of a vicious circle: I can cure you only when you love me, because by loving me you will cure me."

"Always the same prophetic conundrum! But I've already told you that I love you very much!"

"I don't feel it any more than you do. But don't let's talk about that; I am still just a poor monstrous Dragon, an unfortunate Catoblepas."

"If only you would take me on your back, and carry me off to a country where there is some social life. (I'd like so to be launched in society!) And as soon as we arrived, I would pay you for your trouble with a nice little kiss."

"I have already told you that is impossible; our destinies must work themselves out here."

"Do go on, tell me more, won't you?"

"Noble, red-haired Andromeda, I know no more about it than you do."

"Our destinies, our destinies, indeed! But I'm getting older every day! We can't go on like this!"

"Shall we take a little dip?"

"I'm tired of your little dips. It's about time to try something else."

Andromeda throws herself down again on the sand, and rubbing and scratching it alongside her truly famished thighs, emits again her shrill, harsh little moans.

The Monster decides it is time to assume the falsetto voice of this poor pubescent child in order to laugh away her romantic sorrows; and he begins with a tone of complete detachment:

"Pyramus and Thisbe. Once upon a time there was . . ."

"No! No! No more of your deadly stories, or I shall kill myself!"

"Well now, what's this all about? Pull yourself together! Go fishing, hunting, collect rhymes, blow a blast on your conch to the four points of the compass, add to your shell collection; or here, try carving symbols on those recalcitrant rocks (that's the way to kill time!) . . ."

"I can't, I can't; I tell you I've lost my taste for everything."

"Look, child, look up there! Shall I bring you your slingshot?"

This is the third autumnal migration that they have witnessed since dawn; the V passes in one steady rhythmic vibration; there are no stragglers. The birds pass, and by nightfall they will be far away . . .

"If I could only go where they're going! If I could only love, love!" cries poor Andromeda.

The distracted little girl bounds to her feet, and crying into the wind, leaps off and disappears over the gray dunes.

The Monster smiles his debonair smile, and goes back to polishing his pebbles, just as wise old Spinoza must have polished his lenses.

—— II ——

Like a small wounded animal, Andromeda gallops on with the frail leap of a wading bird in a country of ponds, her mad aspect heightened by having incessantly to toss back the long red hair that the wind flattens against her mouth and eyes. Where is she going like that, pubescent girl, through the wind and over the dunes, with the shrieks of a wounded animal?

Andromeda, Andromeda!

With her perfectly shaped feet in their lichen sandals, with a necklace of uncut coral strung on algae-fiber, unabashedly naked and inflexible, she bounds off through wind and sun, water and starlight.

Her face and hands are no whiter than the rest of her body; all her little person, with her silky red hair falling to her knees, is of the same well-bathed terra-cotta color. (Her leaps! Those leaps!)

All elasticity and spring and bronzed by the sun, this wild pubescent girl with her strangely long, delicate legs, her straight proud hips curving in just below the girlish breasts, hints of breasts, so inadequate that her quick breathing as she runs barely lifts them. (When and how could they have been formed, since

she is always forced so against the wind, the salt-wind of the sea
and the furiously cold showers of the waves?) and that long neck,
and that babyish head, so thoroughly pale in its frame of red hair,
with her eyes at times as piercing as those of the sea birds, and at
others as dull as the everyday sea itself. In short, a fully formed
young lady. Oh, those leaps, those leaps, and those cries of a little
wounded girl who has led a hard life! Naked and inflexible and
bronzed by the sun, she has grown like that, with her red hair
flying, against the wind and sun, through water and starlight.

But where is little Pubescence going now?

At the tip of the island, a tall cliff rises on a little promontory;
Andromeda climbs to it through a labyrinth that forms a natural
stairway. From this narrow platform she dominates the island and
the moving silence that isolates it. In the middle of this platform
the rains have hollowed out a basin. Andromeda has lined it with
pebbles of black ivory, and keeps the water clear. This is now her
mirror, and has been, since one fine morning in spring, her only
secret from the world.

For the third time today, she has come back to gaze at herself.
She does not smile into her mirror, she sulks, trying to see into
the depth of her eyes' solemnity; and her eyes never lose their
depth. But her mouth! She does not weary of adoring her mouth's
innocent blossoming. Who will ever understand that mouth?

"How mysterious I look, all the same," she muses.

And then she practices all the expressions she can summon up.

"Well, there I am, just as I am; take me or leave me."

And then she begins to wonder if she isn't basically unap-
pealing!

But she comes back to her eyes. Her eyes are lovely, touching,
and completely hers. She never wearies of making their acquain-
tance; she could stay there and interrogate them until the last
streaks of daylight. What is it about them that keeps them looking
so infinite? Or rather, why isn't she someone else who could
spend her life spying on those eyes, and dreaming of their secret
without talking about it?

But what good does it do to look at herself? Just as she herself is always waiting, so her face, grave and distant, is also waiting.

Then she turns to her red tresses and tries twenty different hair styles, but all of them end up looking too heavy for her little head.

Now some rainclouds come over to disturb her mirror. She keeps, under a stone, a dried fishskin, for use as a nail file. She sits down, and begins to do her nails. The clouds arrive, and break with the sound of a deluge. Andromeda climbs down the cliff, running on toward the sea, crying out to the downpour:

> Ah, for some remedy
> For poor suffering me!
> Some remedy
> For poor little me!

She is so moved by her sad song that tears pour down her child-like breast. And the cloudburst has already moved past, and the wind rumples her hair, and everything is blowing up a squall.

> Yoho! Yoho!
> Since no one will help me — yoho! —
> Into the water I go — I go —
> Yoho!

But it's just for a swim, a simple dip. Then just as she is about to dive into the water, she steps aside. Swimming, always swimming! She is so weary of playing with those vulgarly plump sisters of hers, the waves, about whose complexion and manners she is already abundantly informed. And now she lies down on her back in the wet sand, her arms open to the breakers. It is much easier like this—she has only to wait for a good splash. After a number of threatening waves, a single one arches forward and leaps upon her. With closed eyes, Andromeda receives it stiffly with the cry of one whose neck has been cut, and she twists with all her body to retain this moving icy pillow that breaks up, and leaves her nothing in her arms . . .

She sits down, dazed, and looks at her pitiful, dripping flesh,

and plucks out some strands of algae that this shower has entangled in her hair.

And then she throws herself with determination into the water;
she strikes the waves like a windmill, dives, comes up, takes a
breath, and floats for a while. A new volley of waves arrives, and
now the mad little thing, although knocked flat by them at first,
flops about trying to bestride the crests. She catches one of them
by its mane, and rides it off with her cruel cry; another treacherous one rushes up to unseat her, but then she catches hold of another. And then they all slip away too quickly under her, unable
to wait. But the sea getting excited over the game becomes insupportable; then like flotsam Andromeda lets herself drift disheveled
on the sand: she crawls up beyond the reach of the waves, and lies
there face down in the shifting sand.

Another sheet of rain passes over the island. Andromeda does
not budge; and howling beneath the torrential downpour, she receives the flood, the shrill flood, that plays up and down the little
ravine of her back, stirring up bubbles there. She feels the wet
sand little by little give way under her, and she twists and turns
to dig more deeply into it. (If only I could be completely submerged, buried alive!)

But the torrential stormclouds move off just as they had come,
the noise fades away; the island regains its Atlantic solitude.

Andromeda sits down, and watches the horizon clear up as if
nothing unusual had happened. What can she do now? When the
wind has finished drying her poor little body, she feels rather exhausted, but runs off to scale again the little promontory. There
at least on the cliff some intelligent being, her mirror, awaits her.

But the ugly rain has disturbed the purity of her sad mirror.

Andromeda turns, and is about to burst out sobbing when a
large sea bird dives straight down at the island, the cliff, perhaps
even directly at her. She wails at length for help, sinks back
against the rock, her arms outstretched, and shuts her eyes. Oh, if
only this bird would swoop down upon her little Promethean person, and, perching on her knees, with its impeccably beneficent

beak, begin to draw out the burning core of her little wound.

She feels the enormous wings of the bird fly past, and when she opens her eyes again, it is already far away, drawn undoubtedly by more interesting carcasses. Poor Andromeda, one can readily see that she doesn't know where to take her being so that it may be exorcised.

What can she do now? What can she do if not return to the contemplation of the sea which is so shut in, and which is nevertheless the only opening for hope. Moreover, her unhappiness seems so childish in face of this solitude that stretches farther than the eye can see. With one wave, the sea can quench her thirst forever; and how could she, frail creature that she is, appease or warm the cold sea? She would extend her arms to it in vain . . . And anyway, how tired she is today! Once she used to gallop the whole day long over her domain; now these palpitations of the heart . . . Another of those enormous birds passes over. She would give anything to adopt one of them, to be able to rock it to sleep. But none has ever alighted on the island, and to see them close up, she has to kill them with her slingshot.

To rock to sleep, to be rocked to sleep—the sea is so disobliging in its rocking.

The wind has fallen, the sea is calm, and the horizon lays out a melancholy *tabula rasa* for the ceremony of the setting sun.

To rock, to be rocked! And Andromeda's tired little head is soon filled with lullabies. And she recalls the only lullaby she knows, the legend called "The Truth About Everything," a sacred ditty with which her guardian the Dragon sang her to sleep when she was small:

> In the beginning was Love. Love was the universal law of organization, and it was unconscious and infallible. And Love, being immanent in the interweaving whirlwinds of phenomena, is the infinite aspiration toward the Ideal.
>
> The Sun is the keystone of the Earth's arch, its Reservoir, its Source.

That is why morning and springtime signify happiness, and why twilight and autumn signify death. (And since nothing is more sensitive to superior organisms than to feel themselves dying when they know they aren't, twilight and autumn like the drama of the sun and death constitute the highest aesthetic.)

The Ideal has for ever and ever been sending its impulses through infinite space, continuing to objectify itself in the numberless worlds that are formed and continue their organic evolution as high as their elements will permit, and then disintegrate to begin new hatchings in the laboratory of the Infinite.

The Unconscious has initially nothing to do but climb higher and higher. It occupies itself with watching over new worlds more vivacious and more serious. Nothing will ever distract it from its dreams of tomorrow.

And the Unconscious does not bother with the planets that, having undergone the evolution set off by the Unconscious, have not enough substance left to serve as laboratories for the Being of Tomorrow. Their little evolutions occur fatally as a result of a given impulse like so many worthless, identical copies made from a given and only too well-known negative.

Just as the fetal human evolution in the mother's womb is a miniature reflection of the entire terrestrial evolution, so terrestrial evolution is but a miniature reflection of the Great Unconscious Evolution in Time.

Elsewhere in infinite space the Unconscious is much more advanced. What festivity!

The Earth, if it produced beings superior to Man, would be but a worthless, identical copy of an apprentice's negative. But the good Earth, having descended from the Sun, belongs to us all because we have five senses, and because all Earth responds to them. O succulent morsels, wondrous beauty, perfumes, sounds, surprise as far as the eye can see—O Love, O Life!

Man is but an insect under the heavens; but if he respects himself, then he is indeed God. One spasm from this creature is worth all nature.

Thus Andromeda sullenly intones as another evening falls; and it is easy to recite these lessons that she has learned. She stretches out on the sand and sighs . . . And will go on sighing for how long?

She says in a loud, intelligible voice in the Atlantic solitude of her island:

"Yes, but when some unknown sixth sense wishes to burst forth and nothing, nothing answers it? The truth is that I'm very much alone, left completely to my own resources, and that I'm not at all sure how it will end."

She caresses her arms, then, exasperated, grinds her teeth, scratches herself and slashes her face with a chip of flint she has picked up.

"Still I cannot take my life just to find out, O ye gods!"

She weeps.

"No, no! I am too forsaken. Now they would come in vain to seek me and carry me off; I will bear some resentment, some slight resentment, all my life."

—— III ——

Another evening; another sunset display; the classic, more than classic, schedule.

Andromeda throws back her red hair, and continues on the road to her house.

The Monster does not come to meet her. What does that mean? The Monster is no longer there.

"Monster, monster!" she calls.

No answer. She blows on a conch. Still no answer. She returns to the cliff that dominates the island and blows again and calls. But no! There's no one. She returns home.

"Monster! Monster . . . Oh, disaster! What if he has plunged forever below the water; if he has parted, leaving me alone because I had tormented him and made his life impossible!"

The island in the twilight seems extraordinarily, impossibly lost. She throws herself on the sand in front of her cave, and sobs at length, sobs that she wants to die, that she should have known . . .

When she rises again, the Monster is there, in his habitual muddy outfit, busying himself by piercing holes in the conchs that he fashions into ocarinas for her.

"Well, there you are," she says. "I thought you had left."

"Hardly. As long as I live, I will be your jailer without fear and without reproach."

"What did you say?"

"I said that as long as I live . . ."

"All right, all right; we understand."

Silence and horizon; the horizon of the ocean is swept clear by the setting sun.

"What if we played a game of draughts," Andromeda sighs, her nerves visibly on edge.

"Yes, let's play draughts."

A draughtboard of black and white mosaic stands encrusted at the entrance to the grotto. But hardly has the game begun when Andromeda, her nerves visibly on edge, knocks it over.

"It's impossible, I would lose; my mind wanders constantly. It's not my fault. You can see that my nerves are on edge."

Silence and horizon! After all the wild activities of the afternoon, the air is calm again, having drawn in before the classic retreat of the Sun.

The Sun! . . .

Off there on the flashing horizon where sirens hold their breath,

The scaffolding of the setting sun goes up,

From lighthouse to lighthouse rise vast stage sets;

The pyrotechnists make their final preparations.

Golden moons blossom forth like the mouths of massed trumpets on which the phalanxes of heralds will thunder forth their messages;

The slaughterhouse is ready, the heavy curtains are drawn;

Upon litters of diadems and harvests of Venetian lanterns and piles and sheaves

Backed up by barrages of pinchbeck objects that are already being pilfered,

The Pasha Sun,
His Red Eminence,
In his cassock of collapse,
Descends, mortally triumphant,
For some minutes, down through the Sublime Porte!

And there he lies on his side, completely mottled with atrabilious stigmata.

Someone quickly kicks over this shrunken pumpkinhead, and there you are . . .

Farewell, baskets, the harvest is over.

Rows of trumpets come down, ramparts crumble with the prismatic carafes of the lighthouses! Cymbals fly off, courtiers trip over the standards, tents are folded, the army breaks camp, carrying off in its panic the occidental basilicas, the wine-presses, the idols, the bundles, the vestal virgins, the desks, the ambulances, the bandstands—all the official accessories.

And they all fade into a pink golden dusty haze.

It has all gone beautifully!

"Fabulous, fabulous!" The Taciturn Monster exclaims, driveling with ecstasy, his great watery pupils still lit by the last rays of the setting sun.

"Farewell, baskets; the harvest is done!" Andromeda sighs in her twilit voice, her red-gold hair looking pale indeed after the sunset's conflagration.

"There's nothing left to do but light the evening fires, have supper, and bless the moon, before going to bed and waking tomorrow to another day."

Now silence and horizon are ready for the pale dead moon when—blessed be the gods who see to such things—just at the proper moment a third character appears.

He comes on like a rocket, a hero of diamonds on a Pegasus of snow whose sunset-dipped wings are quivering, sharply reflected in the immense and melancholy mirror offered by the Atlantic on fine evenings.

There is no doubt about it—it is Perseus!

Andromeda, overcome by her maidenly palpitations, runs to hide her face under the Monster's chin.

And large tears come to the Monster's eyes, like candelabra on a balustrade; and he speaks in a voice that we do not at all recognize:

"Andromeda, ah, noble Andromeda. Be calm. This is Perseus, the son of Danaë of Argos whom Zeus visited in a golden shower. He has come to kill me and take you away with him."

"No, he won't kill you!"

"He will kill me."

"If he loves me a little, he will not kill you."

"He can take you away only by killing me."

"No, we shall come to an understanding. People always come to an understanding. I'll take care of it."

Andromeda rises from the place where she usually sits, and looks at him.

"Andromeda, Andromeda, think of the value of your matchless body, think of the value of your virginal soul; a misalliance can be so quickly consummated."

Little does she understand! Gazing straight ahead, arms at her side, hands clenched at her hips, she stands on the bank, still very brave and feminine.

Elegant and miraculous, Perseus approaches. The wings of his hippogriff beat more slowly, and the closer he comes, the more awkward and provincial she feels, not knowing what to do with her lovely arms.

When only a few feet from Andromeda, the perfectly tamed hippogriff stops, kneels at the edge of the waves, supporting himself with his quivering rose-colored wings; and Perseus bows. Andromeda lowers her head. So this is her betrothed. What will his voice be like, what will be his first word?

But then he gallops off without saying anything, and having given himself plenty of space, bounds forward and begins to circle round and round before her, gamboling along the edge of the miraculously mirroring sea, contracting his circles more and more, as if to give this little virgin the time to admire and desire him. It is truly a most unusual spectacle!

This time, smiling, he has passed close enough to touch her.

Perseus is riding sidesaddle, crossing his feet in their sandals of byssus like an elegant horsewoman; a mirror hangs from his saddle; he is beardless, and his mouth is so pink and smiling that it might be mistaken for an open pomegranate; a rose is lacquered on his chest, on his arms are tattooed hearts pierced by arrows, and a lily is painted on the calf of his leg. He wears an emerald monocle, a number of rings and bracelets; from his gilded belt hangs a short sword with a mother-of-pearl hilt.

Perseus wears the helmet of Pluto that renders its wearer invisible; his arms and ankles bear the wings of Mercury, and he carries the divine shield of Pallas Athena. From his belt swings the head of the Gorgon Medusa whose single glance changed the giant Atlas, as we all know, into a mountain, and his hippogriff is Pegasus, which was ridden by Bellerophon when he slew the Chimera. This young hero looks extremely sure of himself.

He reins in, the young hero, before Andromeda, and still smiling like a burst pomegranate, begins to flourish his adamantine sword.

Andromeda does not move. She is apparently ready to weep from uncertainty, ready to give herself up to her destiny as soon as she hears the sound of the hero's voice.

The Monster stands quietly to one side.

With a graceful movement, Perseus turns his mount around, and without disturbing the mirror of the water, makes it kneel before Andromeda and present its side to her. The young knight puts his hands together, and bringing them down like a stirrup before the young captive, and rolling his r's in a most affected manner exclaims:

"To Cythera! Off we go!"

So it's settled; Andromeda places her rough foot in this delicate stirrup, and then turns to wave farewell to the Monster. But the latter dives between them under the hippogriff and rears up on the other side, his paws held forth, showing the purplish blue cavern of his jaws from which darts a knife of flame. The hippogriff is frightened; Perseus draws back to give himself ample room and makes boastful, blustering noises. The Monster faces him; Perseus darts forward, then stops, abruptly, saying:

"No, I won't give you the pleasure of being killed before her eyes," he exclaims, "fortunately the just gods have provided more than one string to my bow. I will . . . turn you to stone."

The little darling of the gods unhooks from his belt the head of the Gorgon Medusa.

Cut off at the throat, the celebrated head is still living, throbbing with a stagnant and poisoned life; it is black with suppressed apoplexy, its blank, bloodshot eyes fixed straight ahead, and fixed its decapitated grin, nothing stirring on it but the serpents that cover its head like hair.

Perseus seizes it by this hair, the blue gold-mottled curls of which add further bracelets to his wrists, and holds it out to the Dragon. To Andromeda he cries out, "Turn your eyes away!"

But miraculously the charm does not work.

The charm did not want to work.

Indeed, with an unprecedented effort, the Gorgon Medusa has closed her petrifying lids.

The amiable Medusa has recognized our Monster. She remembers the rich and lovely breeze-swept days when she and her sisters lived with this Dragon. It was he who then watched over the wonderful garden of the Hesperides, which is situated near the Pillars of Hercules. No, a thousand times no, she will certainly not turn her old friend to stone.

Perseus is still waiting, his arms extended, unaware of anything unusual. The contrast between his brave and masterful gesture and its failure to come off is rather grotesque; and the wild little Andromeda has not been able to restrain herself from smiling.

Perseus notices the smile on her lips. The hero is astonished: What on earth has happened to his fine Medusa Head? And although his helmet makes him invisible, it is not without a certain fear that he dares to gaze upon the Gorgon's face, to be sure of what is happening there. It is very simple: the petrifying charm of the Medusa has not worked because the Gorgon has closed her eyes.

Perseus is furious; he hangs the head back in place and brandishes his sword with a conqueror's laugh. And holding the divine shield of Pallas Athena in front of his heart, he digs his spurs in (at the very moment while over there the full moon is rising on the miraculous Atlantic mirror) and swoops down on the poor wingless Dragon. He corners him with dazzling maneuvers, stabs him on the right and then on the left, and then finally backs him up against a crag and sinks his sword so splendidly right in the middle of the Monster's forehead that the poor Dragon collapses. As he dies, he has only time to say: "Farewell, noble Andromeda; I loved you, and if you had wished, there would have been some future to my love. Farewell; you will think of me often."

The Monster is dead. And although his victory was inevitable, Perseus is so excited that he continues to attack the dead creature; he stabs him again and again, puts out his eyes, and continues the butchery until Andromeda stops him.

"Enough, enough. Can't you see that he is dead?"

Perseus slips his sword back into his scabbard, draws back his blond curls, swallows a mint, and dismounts, patting Pegasus's neck.

"And now, my beauty," he says in a slightly drunken way.

Andromeda, still standing there irrepoachably and unabashedly naked with her black seagull eyes, asks:

"Do you love me? Do you really love me?"

"Do I love you? I absolutely adore you, and life without you would be insupportable, terrifying! Do I love you? Just look at yourself!"

And he holds out his mirror to her, but Andromeda, seemingly overcome with surprise, pushes it back. Paying no heed to her gesture, he hastens to add:

"Oh, come on! We want to look our best, don't we?"

He takes off one of his necklaces, a necklace made of gold coins (a souvenir of his mother's golden bridegroom) and tries to slip it around her throat. She gently pushes away the necklace, but he takes advantage of her gesture by putting his arms around her waist. The little wounded creature awakens. Andromeda utters a cry, the cry of gulls on their worst days, a cry that echoes throughout the already dark island.

"Don't touch me! . . . I am sorry, but really all this has happened so quickly. Please let me wander around a little. I must say farewell to everything here."

She turns away and embraces the whole island, clasping to her breast the beloved cliff on which night is falling—night so serious and elusive with respect to her whole future that Andromeda turns quickly toward the one who has come to wrench her away from her past, toward the one who holds all the stakes in her future. And she surprises him yawning. He tries to cover up his yawn with that burst-pomegranate smile of his.

O night on the island of the past! Monster treacherously slain and denied burial. The far too elegant countries that await her in the future. All Andromeda can do is cry out:

"Go away! Go away! I have a horror of you. Go away, and leave me to die alone; you have come to the wrong island."

"What a fine way to behave! Believe me, little one, people of my sort don't have to be given orders like that twice. In my eyes, you have already lost your looks."

He flourishes his adamantine sword, gets back in his saddle, and flies off into the enchantment of the rising moon, without turning around; she hears him yodeling a sweet melody as he flashes off like a meteor toward more elegant and comfortable countries.

O night on the poor quotidian island! What a dream! . . .

Andromeda stands there with her head lowered, gazing bewildered at the horizon, the magic horizon that she did not want, that she could not want, thanks to the great heart that you have given her, oh, gods.

She walks toward the Monster, the poor Monster lying, purplish and flaccid, on the sand. What a waste, really!

She tries to lie down under his chin as she has always done, but now that he is dead, she must lift it up and put her small arms around his neck. His body is still warm. Carefully, with one finger she lifts up one eyelid, the eyelid reveals a crushed eye, and closes again over it. She pushes back the hair of his mane, and counts the bleeding holes that the ugly glittering sword has made. And tears for the past and tears for the future, tears for the silence that emanates from him flow from her eyes. How beautiful life on this island had been with him! And running her fingers automatically through his long eyelashes, she recalls what a good friend—accomplished gentleman, hard-working scholar, and eloquent poet—he had been. And her little heart breaks into sobs, and she writhes under the inert chin of the much misunderstood Monster. She clasps her arms around his neck, and swears all the things that she did not swear when he was still alive.

"Poor, poor Monster! Why didn't you tell me that all this was going to happen? You would not have been killed by this ugly comic-opera hero. And I wouldn't have been left all alone in the dark! We would still have some happy days together. You should have seen that my infatuation, my fatal curiosity was but a passing thing. O thrice fatal curiosity. I've killed my only friend, my foster father, my preceptor. Now with what lamentations I could make these cold shores resound. Noble Monster, his last words were for me: 'Farewell, Andromeda; I loved you, and if you had wished, there would have been a future to our love!' How well I now understand the greatness of your soul—and your silences, your afternoons and all. Too late, too late! But still all this must have been ordained by the gods. Oh, just gods, take half of Andromeda's life, take half of my life and give me back his so that

I may love him and serve him henceforth gently and faithfully. Oh, gods, do that for me, you who can read my heart and know deep down how I loved him, even when momentarily blinded by the vagaries of adolescence, and know that I have never loved anyone but him, and that I will always love him!"

And noble Andromeda passes the lovely bloom of her lips over the Dragon's closed eyelids. And suddenly she recoils from him.

For at her prophetic words and her redeeming tears, the Monster trembles, opens his eyes, weeps in silence, and gazes at her. Then he says:

"Noble Andromeda, I thank you. Our ordeal is over. I am reborn, and I am going to be born into a body that can love you properly. And there will be no words on earth to describe your great happiness. But I must tell you who I am, and what my destiny has been. I was of the cursed race of Cadmus, dedicated to the Furies. I preached the absurdity of existence and the divinity of oblivion in the flowering fields of Arcadia. To punish me the gods of life changed me into a Dragon, and condemned me to guard the treasures of this earth until a virgin came to love me, monstrous being, for myself. Three-headed Dragon, I guarded at length the golden apples of the garden of Hesperides. Hercules came there and slit one of my throats. Then I went to Colchis, to await the arrival of the Golden Fleece. Phryxus of Thebes and his sister Helle set out for Colchis, riding on the ram with the Golden Fleece. According to an oracle, Helle was the promised virgin. But she drowned on the way, and gave her name to the Hellespont. (I have learned since that she was not very pretty.) And then came those strange magnificent Argonauts, creatures of the sort one will never see again. O splendid epochs! Jason was their leader, Hercules followed with his friend Theseus, and Orpheus who undertook to delight me on his lyre (and who was, of course, to meet such a tragic end); Castor, the celebrated tamer of horses, also came, and his twin brother Pollux, who was equally celebrated as a boxer. But those glorious days are over! And the divine bivouacs, and the campfires they lit in the evening. Finally I had my second head cut off in front of the Golden Fleece of the Holy Grail, thanks to my being drugged by the philters of Medea, who burned with love for the sumptuous Jason. And the cycles began again. I knew Eteocles and Polynices, and the pious Antigone. And the perfection of armaments that brought an end to the Golden Age. And then at last I knew that strange, lush, and overpowering Ethiopia, and your father and you, noble Andromeda, more beautiful than all the others, and whom it is my destiny to be able to make so happy that no words on earth will be able to describe your happiness."

As soon as he completed this eloquent discourse, the Dragon, without a word of warning, was changed into a perfect young man. Leaning on a rock at the entrance to the grotto, his human skin bathed in the enchanting moonlight, he speaks of the future.

Andromeda does not dare to recognize him, and turning away, smiles into the void, with one of those flashes of sadness that always accompany her impulsive actions (for her soul is always so quickly overcome.)

But one must indeed live out this life, no matter how wide-eyed it may make one at each turning of the road.

The morning after this most nuptial night, they dug a canoe from the trunk of a tree and launched it on the waves.

And off they sailed, avoiding the coasts studded with casinos. Oh, honeymoon under the sun and under the stars!

And on the third day they reached the coast of Ethiopia, the kingdom of Andromeda's disconsolate father. (You can imagine his joy.)

"Well, my dear Monsieur Amyot de l'Épinal, you're going a little bit too far with that story of yours," cried the Princess d'U. . . , drawing her shawl around her shoulders, for the evening, splendid though it was, was cool. "I gave my heart in quite another way to that story of Perseus and Andromeda. I shan't quibble with the caricature you have drawn of that poor Perseus. (But I forgive you only because of the masterly and flattering way in which you have depicted me as Andromeda). But the denouement leaves much to be desired! What's the sense of this Monster, to whom no one until now has paid the slightest attention? And then, dear Monsieur Amyot de l'Épinal, just lift your eyes for a moment to the map of the heavens. Look at that pair of nebulae over there near Cassiopeia. Isn't that what they call Perseus and Andromeda? And look at that crooked outcast line of stars down there below—isn't that the constellation called the Dragon, which leads such a wretched existence there between the Great Bear and the Little Bear, those two related constellations that look so like unlicked cubs?"

"My dear U. . . , that doesn't prove a thing. The heavens are calm and conventional. One might as well say that your eyes are simply brown. You wouldn't like that, would you? No, can't you also see, down there, near the Lyre, which is my constellation, the Swan, which is the constellation of Lohengrin and has the form of a cross in memory of Parsifal? And yet wouldn't you admit that my Lyre and I have nothing whatever to do with Lohengrin and Parsifal?"

"That's true, that's true, if only parabolically. But it's impossible to discuss anything properly with you, or to learn anything from you. Let's go in and have tea. And, by the way, what is the moral of the story; I always forget the moral?"

"Here it is:

> Young ladies, look quite carefully
> Before you decide to turn up your nose
> At some poor Monster; this fable shows
> He may well be the happiest one of three."

PAN AND THE SYRINX
or the Invention of the Reed-pipe

On his poor little morning pipe Pan plays out his very personal sorrows to the echoing Valley-of-the-Dappled-Green in Arcadia.

We have all been on such a lovely summer morning in such a joyfully marvelous valley, and we all can say that we know exactly what it's like.

In the blessedly virginal expanse, the springlike cataracts of sunlight in radiant mists of happiness, in a mossy flood of champagne infused with the Sun itself, bathe the thick woodland and the spread of hills and the entire valley. Oh, myriad prisms of optimism! Oh, Youth, oh, Beauty, oh, Unanimity! Oh, Sunlight! . . .

Young and immortal, Pan has never loved, as he and I understand the word.

During the whole night, in a valley flooded with a memorable moon solo, he bitterly blew on his imperfect, monotonous pipe, his poor little two-penny pipe. Then he finally went off to sleep, and his dreams made his heart all the emptier. At dawn he stretched out his hairy goat legs curly with dew (he has given up calisthenics); and now lying face down on his elbows in the thyme, alone in the delicate morning solitude, he has begun to tootle his frustration to himself on his pipe that has only four notes. What can you do when you're in *love* if not wait around like this in the open air and try by means of art to express yourself?

Pan waits a while and then sings:

> The Other Sex! The Other Sex!
> Oh, little Eve—
> See her whole,

As she advances, thrilled with her role,
Eyes gleaming,
Of wedlock dreaming,
Hair tumbling down
In the holy dawn.

Look, look,
Look at little Eve, who down the slope now rushes
With her sacrificial flesh
And her soul covered with blushes! . . .

A body, a soul,
A childhood friend at my side,
A woman born
To be my bride!

See how quickly she comes,
A lump in her throat,
Pink honey her gums,
Breasts as timid as leverets! . . .

With breezes playing under
Her red-cherry earrings,
Lifting her little nose,
Crying to the sun, "Oh, you Wonder!"

Then, posing proudly and proclaiming:
"I am no little peahen,
I am no doll;
I have freed myself from all
To run aground on the heart of the Great God Pan!
As pure as a tulip'll
Ever be, free of principle!
April, April,
My happiness hangs by a thread!"

Flora and fauna—
Lest we forget—
Show us our duties
From sunrise to sunset.

> I saw her in a dream,
> My welcome little Eve.
> Ah, what an epiphany
> Genius has worked for me!

Pan stops singing and turns his eyes again to the blessedly virginal morning in the whole valley. What a radiant morning it is
with all the sunlight and all that elusive universal happiness! And
there you have it: it's up to him to arrange to be happy just as
this morning has arranged to be happy.

Easier said than done. Pan indulges again in his pipe, which, although imperfect, is faithful and worthy of being called a true
buddy. He begins the ancient ballad, "I've been disgusted with
wild strawberries," and then breaks off at once, disgusted with
the ballad itself.

But never mind! Between his legs thyme quivers, bees hum,
stems of umbels relax completely in the lovely air, cicadas begin
to roast with cries of pleasure: as far as the eye can see, happiness
reigns!

Pan, feeling that he, too, has a reason for being, gives a more
human touch to the *ritornello* based on his great passion:

> My soul makes my body ache,
> My body makes my soul ache.
> Like a stag I bell as I lie awake,
> And nothing has turned up yet.
>
> Her flesh would not be all to me,
> And I wouldn't be just Pan to her.
> Together let us play it cool
> Rather than having to play the fool.

Then he reasons with himself in a little aside:

"Oh, Woman, Woman! Creator of monomaniac humanity! I
love you, I love you! But what is this word *love?* What does it
come from and what does it add up to with its neutral, inconsequential syllable? Here is what I make of it: *Love* says something

to me only when I associate with its sound. It's not just whimsical to remember that the English word *aim* means *goal* and the French word *aime* means *love*. I love you—*Je t'aime*—then would mean, 'I aim toward you, you are my goal.' And so if I've got it right, fine! That's great!

> You will come soon, won't you?
> Where shall I seek you,
> My fragile Psyche,
> Whom each instant must deflower
> Far from my prosperous arms?
>
> Yes, it will be wholly you!
> And cleverly I'll lead you
> Into the depth of the woods,
> To the coolest part;
> And there you will lie on the grass,
> After so many virginal afternoons,
> And give yourself up to summer
> With the deafening sound of cicadas.
>
> You will see, you will see
> That I am not ungrateful,
> That my arms are rich
> And fertile as the earth.
> And it's not your flesh which . . .

"Ssh! Here she is! Laughing and white, coming through the tall grass of my meadow! Let's sing something and pretend to be completely absorbed in our song so as not to frighten her. Good heavens, yes, let her come!

> I've been disgusted with wild strawberries
> Since I dreamt of my little Eve.
> Since I saw her smile at me
> With a finger to her lips.
>
> I must say that I've been disgusted with mystery
> Since my naughty little Eve

Smiled so invitingly
And signaled to me
To keep quiet! . . .

Mystery and smile,
Oh, my lovely dream-boat!

Smile, and be mute.
Be still, my lute!

And, on my word, *her flesh would not be everything to me.*"

Right through the full morning, in the holy sunlight, through the happy meadow, here indeed is the nymph Syrinx advancing, quite unexpected in the full actuality of her flesh and bones (with what youth her wide eyes swear to it!). She has paused here, with a delighted gaze, neck arching forward, arms swinging, wholly charmed by the inoffensive plaint of Pan. Little by little, in order to hear him better, she has sat down in the pretty thyme opposite him but at some distance—at some discreet distance.

Yes, there she truly is, pink and modest, waiting as lovely as an almond tree in bloom.

She is not ashamed, and knows her worth, which can't be judged by any ordinary measure. But with her thick hair swept up into a very personal diadem, her large eyes elevated toward elevation and her delicate little pink pout, she hardly seems to realize that she is in the world to give herself up like this to summer with the deafening sound of cicadas.

And yet, in spite of her large eyes elevated toward elevation and her hair done up in a diadem and her very distinguished pout, she was born, equipped, to come to such an end.

"Yes," Pan whispers.

"Alas," Pan whispers, "come what may, she'll have tomorrow or the day after those same wide superhuman clear eyes of hers and that pout emanating from another world."

But what difference does it make! Pan has, in the course of his meditations, run up against more than one such irreducible para-

dox. And today, sick and overpowered with love as he is, he
would without any argument accept Woman as she is.

He has stopped playing his little trills. He gazes at *her*. He does
not yet dare to speak for fear of breaking the charm of this apparition, which he does not after all deserve. Better to let himself get
it throughly into his mind that she is there and that all this is
actually happening.

They gaze at each other. He, his teeth clenched, his eyes filled
with sadness, she, her wide, clear eyes and the mouth of a child
spoiled by higher things, and perfectly overwhelmed with being
just as she is, with neither ups nor downs.

So it is she who takes it upon herself to break the spell—because
there really is a spell. Her voice is decidedly slow and nostalgic,
but unshakably clear.

"That's a very pretty piece you're playing."

"Oh, this is just a two-penny pipe. If I had a proper reed-pipe,
I could really play. I'd be absolutely sure of myself! . . ."

She is quiet again, her attention fixed on the lovely weather.

"I'd be absolutely sure," Pan insists, "even of . . ."

"Of what?"

"Even of having you share the love that I've felt for so long."

"Really?"

This "really" is spoken in a proper, but quite unworldly, way.
And without lowering her eyes, she starts to smooth the pleats of
her short tunic, the pleats of her short white tunic stretched tight
below her young breasts and caught with a clasp on one shoulder.

"Really?"

"Yes, but I know there's no use trying. Your eyes are so big,
and that pout is so charming. No. And then, anyway, this morning I have too bad a headache. But thank you for having come.
Your presence is very restful."

She is silent, with her clear eyes, and the day is truly magnificent.

Pan lowers his head, and amuses himself by slashing small flowers and blades of grass.

He raises his eyes. She is still there, resting in the thyme, still contemplating him with her virginally intelligent look and her virginally intelligent pout.

No. No one can have quite such an innocent look as that.

"When will you have done?"

"Done with what?"

This "Done with what?" is spoken with such an intensification of the perfection of her eyes and her pout that Pan begins to writhe and emits in the radiant morning solitude a long and unique sigh of love, of absolute Pan-ic love.

But she must know where his sigh came from and where it is bound for, since the perfection of her manner is not at all disturbed by it! . . .

Pan, who already pictured her as completely frightened and had an "Oh, don't be afraid!" ready to deal with the situation, merely says:

"I'm sick, so sick. I know you very well. You're going to insist indignantly that you were just passing this way, that you just happened by. What do you know about it all? How did you happen to be passing by? You don't say anything. I wouldn't be ungrateful. But then, let's drop it."

He lowers his head and begins again to slash blades of grass and small flowers like a raving madman. He raises his eyes: she gazes at him with her whole beauty that seems decidedly pointless. What if he threw his immortal body at her feet to dazzle her! But he restrains himself. What must happen will happen; everything is part of Everything. And he takes up his pipe again, his old worn-out pipe, with the air of a young man for whom art, and a scale or two a day, are all that is required.

He begins chimerically to warble:

> Lovely eyes gleaming,
> Of wedlock dreaming!
> Soul that blushes suddenly,
> Flesh oiled with the wrong scent.

Her flesh would not be all to me
And I wouldn't be just Pan to her.
Together let us play it cool
Rather than having to play the fool.

April! April! (here a painful *ritardando*)
Our happiness hangs by a thread!

Epiphany! Epiphany!
My genius in its entirety!

Enough exercise for one morning. Pan lifts his head. She's still there, smiling, as if wholly disarmed by this great big boy, and a bit by the exceptional beauty of the morning.

Pan would have only to answer this smile by a simple honest smile of his own. But he finds it more to the point to shrug his shoulders and assume a superior dilettante air.

"What astonishing eyes you have, upon my word, you, whoever you are! And that face descending to such a charming point, and that justifiable pout! Do you ever dream of looking any other way when you gaze in the mirroring spring water?"

"No, indeed! Since we all have the faces our souls give us, my soul couldn't conceive of itself any better than in my face. It's a vicious circle, of just the kind you like."

"It's fortunate that you are a goddess: if you weren't, you would be an old woman one day, and your soul would then conceive a face rather different from its own."

"I hadn't thought of that. You are certainly a realist."

"I am Pan."

"Pan who?"

"I am . . . well, not much at the moment, but in general I am Everything, if ever there was anything. Don't you understand, I am both the song of the wind . . ."

"And what about Aeolus, then?"

"No, listen. I am things, the life of things, in the classic sense, in one sense. No, I am nothing. Ah, how wretched I am! If only

I had an instrument a bit more complicated than this two-penny pipe, I would play out for you all that I am. I would sing fantastically! Classic sobriety makes me laugh! I would sing many a *Kyrie* and *Gloria in excelsis,* as well as the graceful, lively songs of my native land."

"But you know men can't ever be simple with women. They should always declare themselves in good straightforward language, in the light and noble Ionic dialect. But no, they have to have music at once, music because it's so universally infinite . . ."

Pan rises, furious:

"And what about you! The very sound of a woman's voice is music—so isn't that cheating already? Oh, dear, it's all rather sad—for both of us really."

He rolls over in the thyme at her feet, like some wretched Caliban, and moans. She looks him over with her wide, compassionate, yet distinguished, eyes.

Pan recovers; and says in a superior way:

"In short, noble virgin, whoever you are, you have a body much like those that I've seen before. It's getting late in the day, and I have never loved. Will you be everything to me, in the name of Everything?"

A pause (time lost while the whole countryside continues its happy existence).

In all her loveliness, the nymph Syrinx slowly rises to her feet. She says quietly:

"I am the Nymph Syrinx. I'm a bit of a naiad, too, for my father of the handsome torso and the flowering beard is the river Ladon. I was just coming down from Mount Lycaeus. . ."

"Aha! A naiad, then! You must find me rather ugly, very much a Caliban, very goatlike. A naiad! A cousin of the handsome Narcissus, the son of the River Cephisus. Bless my soul! He was handsome, Narcissus, wasn't he? And distinguished, too."

The nymph Syrinx stiffens, throws back a lock of hair from her wide forehead, and declares brusquely and coolly:

"You are quite mistaken. I am an esthetic soul, dipped seven times in the cold waters of the Castalian spring, dear to the chaste muses. I am the most loyal of Diana's cohorts. . ."

Pan recoils. Syrinx raises her arms toward the pure firmament where Hecate will shine this evening; with this gesture, her two pale breasts, under her diaphanous tunic, pure and lunar, sink back as they rise:

"O Diana! Empress of pure nights! The membranes of your heart are as rough as the tongues of your hounds. You leap across streams, and you say little. Your steely gaze staunches the pink blood of young ladies who would like to take at once to their beds. The pleats of your chlamys are purely Doric. Returning from your hunting expeditions, one falls like a dirty log on a pile of dry leaves and sleeps a dreamless sleep until the fanfare of dawn. On with the hunt! On with the hunt!"

Syrinx emits the strident laugh of a Walkyrie, and, forgetting Pan, begins to race, young and bounding, over hill and dale, through the lovely morning.

And Pan, his heart broken by a vast primitive sadness, watches her depart without glancing back. He stands there, suddenly defeated and wretched as if the whole state of the wretchedness and filth in which we live had been revealed to him. How pure she is as she leaps forward, staring straight ahead. Poor Pan! He has just felt in his heart like a lightning flash the great and legendary sorrow of Ceres as she goes over the whole earth, a dusty beggar, interrogating all the shepherds, seeking her daughter Proserpine who had disappeared one morning while gathering a bouquet of wild flowers for her mother.

Love, love, would you have me dry up here without a word, without a verse?

But Pan is immortal! And at the thought of this melancholy evening, alone with his genius, at the thought of the sublime discussions by which he would charm Diana herself, Pan inhales the open air that belongs to everyone and dashes off in pursuit of the precious fugitive! On with the hunt!

And the legendary pursuit of the nymph Syrinx by the god Pan in Arcadia begins. Oh, what an adventure!

He will catch her. He will bring her to her knees in some corner of the wood, and tell her just what he thinks of her; he will turn her into a creature no better than he is and then be able to adore her with all his great, misunderstood heart!

She is already far away. She turns around and sees that she is being followed. She pauses for a moment, facing him; then dashes off madly again.

"Ah, you're running away, are you? I'll catch you! I'll take hold of your little wrists and grind your little cat bones to powder, I'll teach you! . . ."

Oh, long and legendary day, you are far from us now, and you'll never return! . . . All this happened in Arcadia before the coming of the Pelasgians.

The sunshine is everywhere, the fields are rapturous, the birds are warbling merrily away throughout the countryside, and there are flowering shrubs everywhere to catch the eye! Deer in pairs lift their heads from the stream; on the perpendicular rocks goats pause in their browsing; and along the edges of the wood are squirrels in the dry leaves taking sudden little leaps, broken by vast intervals of silence.

When he has conquered and tamed this superhuman little savage, they will come one day to wander by this place, and he will make her suffer over the color of a leaf, he will never be adequately avenged.

Meanwhile, on with the hunt! On with the hunt! Through the whole morning!

Syrinx will maintain her lead for some time, since she is not exhausted by insomnia or fever, has not given up the practice of calisthenics, has slept well, and lives a regular life. While they are still on the plain, all goes well; but when they skirt a wood, Syrinx amuses herself from time to time by darting in and out of the trees, and Pan must stop to see if this is not a trick and if she is not about to leave the main road and start across the wood.

"I'll catch you, I'll catch you! And then I'll sit and sulk for three days and nights. Oh, how I love you! You are my goal. How lovely your flight is! And how my brute Caliban heart lights up at each minute of your flight, and what lovely tears I'll shed for you this evening, once I've forgiven you."

After passing a few fields and woods and other scenes, Syrinx finds herself facing a steep bank covered with flowering brambles. She turns and ascends this obstacle from one side, up a gentle slope, then turns to stand on the height within sight of Pan, who still runs straight ahead. She watches him approach. And Pan, instead of taking the bank from an angle as she has, founders at the foot of the ravine. He stops. An armistice will be declared while he continues to gaze up at her. (Let him at least take in the present reality!) They will undoubtedly now continue their discussion, and perhaps it will end amicably under the midday sun.

How irresistibly, in that noble and still quivering pose, she towers over him from high up there. And her whole chaste, sweet appearance, with the diadem of her hair undisturbed, and her large clear eyes as unruffled by insomnia as the surface of a stream by a rose's perfume. How pure and perfect her legs are up there!

"Why are you pursuing me?" she cries, in a voice that is accustomed to calling and commanding Diana's hounds.

"Because I love you—*je t'aime;* you are my *aim*—my goal!" he replies in his most Pantheistic voice.

In his most Pantheistic voice! But Syrinx, Diana's companion, is a spiritualist, and so must have her own ideas on reproduction and all that.

"Do you take me for an animal, a little classified animal? Do you know that I am priceless?"

"And I, I am an artist, someone remarkable! But, deep down, my soul is the soul of a great shepherd—you'll see."

"Please understand this—my pride in remaining myself is as great as my miraculous beauty! Although I've not forgotten how, at times, to be a child. . ."

"Oh, Syrinx, gaze on the Earth and understand it. Gaze on this marvelous morning and all the movement of life. You, there! I, here! Oh, you! I! Everything is part of Everything!"

"Everything part of Everything! Really. Oh, these people who live by formulas! Why not sing to me of my beauty?"

"Yes, of course."

She stands up there, firmly in place, with an air of indefinite good spirits. Pan climbs a tree, facing her, but not within reach, and sits on a branch, his legs dangling down.

He begins, gazing into her eyes in peaceful meditation.

"Most immaculate conception! . . . No, it's no good. I'll not be able to come up with anything else."

"I'm still waiting; it will only be a game, of course. When will you tell me of my beauty if not now? Look me over closely, closely. Be good for something, be my mirror just as human consciousness tries to be the mirror of the undefined Ideal. . ."

"Ah, not like that, my ideal child. That would give you too great a claim to all that is imperceptible. (A pedant deserves a more than pedantic answer.)"

"I'm just recognizing in passing that happiness has nothing to do with the pursuit of the Ideal, nothing at all."

"That I can only answer with a rude remark."

"Go ahead."

"You are putting the question, the aim of the discussion, in the wrong way. You are not the aim of my pursuit; under the guise of aim, you are but one stage between us. Which amounts to the same thing in any case: since so long as I do not know you, you are for me my very aim itself, the Ideal. When I've reached the stage where you are and crossed it, however absolute it may be, I'll be able to see beyond it. (One more than pedantic deserves the complete truth!)"

"It's clear. I might well constrain you to wait forever before the illusion of my domain or to leap across it. But no, I only wish like you to be a victim of our mutual illusion. Describe to me at least first of all my appearance as illusion."

"Well . . . Most Immaculate Conception. I close my eyes, and your wide eyes are already there like immortally attentive souls. Diana's holy bow possesses no inflection more definite than the bow of your mouth. Oh, do not unbend it. Your wide eyes announce something that I shall call Christianity, and you hold your head high like one who gazes above the flocks of Pan to see if the Messiah has not yet come."

Syrinx has sat down on the bank, her legs dangling in the brambles, her perfect, lovely legs and her feet in their white sandals. She leans on her right elbow, her head in her hand, gazing out with her wide nostalgic and unexplored eyes.

Pan continues to mumble his platitudes.

"Everything is in Everything! And little Syrinx is a product of the Earth. But how can I love you and describe your beauty at the same time? Wait for me. I'm going to join you. No, stay where you are. You are beautiful, spontaneously perfect!

"Your organs express the price of natural immortality. We shall run in perpetual betrothal through the brambles of the mountains. How lovely you must be while you are hunted down!"

"On with the hunt!" cries Syrinx, who deified by this cry, has leapt to her feet and continues to run toward the light, emitting cries like those of the Walkyries:

> Hoyo—toho!
> Heia—ha!
> Ha—hei! Hei—aho! Hoyo—hei!

They must start all over again. Before climbing down from this pitiful tree, Pan must watch to see which direction the lovely girl will take. Then he must go back and climb this bank by the gentle slope. But indignation fires him with primitive ardor. Caliban awakens in him. He emits the hoarse bark of a poor bewildered bear that has been made to perform too long! The little girl with her divine leaps has a head start, but now it's just a matter of time!

And the great god Pan's legendary pursuit of the nymph Syrinx continues through the oppressive afternoon that will before long melt into evening. . .

A woman she is, that much is sure! And he will catch her! At the latest, he will catch her over there atop that bluish hill, or in the depth of the valley beyond, and he will frighten her deep within a damp and slippery grotto that he knows well. Everything is Everything, and he will force her to cry *Aditi!* After all, he will be the one who ends up asking her pardon, but that doesn't matter. Ah, Diana-Artemis can rise this evening with her pale discobolus; she will see some fine things. It's not for nothing that Everything is in Everything.

They cross great pine forests of kilometrically cloistered solitude where it has been dark since the beginning of the world, when God said: "Let there be light!" And the divine child, as she leaps, fills these grandiose corridors with her intractable cries:

> Hoyotoho!
> Heiaha!
> Hahei!   Heiaho!   Hoyohei!

"O cries of glory and happiness! How well she understands me! On with the hunt! Oh, now I understand—you can be happy only when at bay with bleeding feet. Come, I will staunch the blood of your heroic feet and bathe your pure, perfect limbs and, humming *Aditi*, rock you all night long. Atop the blue hill we shall light our evening fires. And that will be for ever and for every day. And all Olympus will speak of the genius of Pan and of his up-to-date love affairs. How delightful she will be in the coming autumn amid the falling leaves that no one yet has been able to fathom! Oh, for that season I must perfect my pipe and let it sing out the first snows of things as they are. *Hoyotoho!* Run on; run on forever. Night has not yet fallen."

And to allow his fiancée a little breathing space, Pan, having reached the top of a hill overlooking a new plain, pauses. The fiancée turns around for a moment, startled. Has he had enough? Does he want to give up this game? Unsure, she runs off again. *Hoyotoho!* Night has not yet fallen.

At a certain point in the field stands a tomb's dazzling white marble block. Syrinx pauses beside it, and, leaning over it as if to smell a flower, utters her mocking *Heiaha!* and with her divine leaps continues her lovely flight. . .

Heiaha, indeed! Pan runs down the little hill and continues the equally divine leaps of his pursuit! . . .

He in turn pauses for a moment beside the white marble tomb. Like the object of his pursuit, he leans over; there are no flowers to smell, only this inscription on which to meditate:

ET IN ARCADIA EGO

"And I also lived in Arcadia! Poor mortals, how many reasons they have for loving one another!"

But Pan and Syrinx are immortal, so there is no hurry.

The plain stretches away as far as the blue hill, as vast as an afternoon that will melt into evening. The *Hoyotoho* and *Heiaha* become less frequent. What a plain! . . .

What a plain! . . .

And slowly, since everything follows its natural course, the sun sinks. The poor nymph feels twilight start to weave the invisible thread of its net. Syrinx loses ground; and the blue hill will soon be there, hedged in undoubtedly with terrible brambles. Oh, in the brambles she'll climb as long as she can, covered with blood, and how sorry he will feel. . . .

"She is weakening, weakening! But she doesn't want to give up! She takes me for a lecherous Caliban. But I will kneel down before her and staunch the blood on her feet!—I will touch her hair, and run my fingers several times over her delicate arm and make her attend to me! I'll win her with gentleness and fatalistic concern. And I'll also have to see about dinner. Oh, I'll confound her with all my little contradictory attentions. . . And she will weep and sob out her infinite forgiveness."

This is the twilight hour. . .

The sun bids farewell, or rather says *au revoir*, and without making a fuss (these were the good old days after all). The landscape begins to shiver, languishing with belated loving-care.

The poplar, a most refined tree with perfect timing, trembles. And the weeping willow weeps for the unreasonable clouding over of its mirroring waters. The hills and distances darken with uneasy solitude. The tree frogs will begin to sing again, and the stars will not—could not—delay coming out. Nothing is lacking but the angelus. (Other times, other ways.) Oh, twilight! Innocence and fraternity by the grace of God. A time for wayside worship, is it not? A time for the Unknown to remain unknown, and peace on earth for couples of good will.

Oh, sheaves of a harvested *past*, so-called native land, false convalescence! Soon it will be night; the glowworm will do his work, and the owl speak his word.

But, thank heaven, it is still light, and the young lady still holds out and swears that she will make it up the next slope, however slightly that may delay the splitting of her life in two.

She is familiar with this twilight that strangles these *Heiaha*'s in her throat. She knows that once the net of evening has been cast, nothing less than the moonlight of watchtowering Diana, with the full flood of her beams, will be needed to cleanse all these ambulations. She goes on, and reaches the hill. . .

"Oh, twilight, you do not touch me, you will never touch me! Strong, sensual pleasure will never filter through the ciborium of my being!—But who was that whispering over there? . . ."

Alas, three times alas, what is whispering there behind the reeds is a treacherous little stream: shadowy and deep, it encircles the hill. Shadowy water stretching into the evening. . .

Syrinx parts the reeds and sees the stream, wide and deathly quiet. And Pan arrives! Man, drunk with night!

He stands there some distance away; Syrinx turns and lifts her hand to him!

How lovely she is thus in the evening! What is he to think? . . .

"Will you put me out of your mind?"

"I'm sorry, but there's nothing I can do about it. Put you out of my mind! I love you, you are my aim, I am I, and night is falling! Don't worry, I'll explain everything. What is there about me that so disgusts you? Together at last! Isn't every part of your body breathing in this summer night? Oh, summer night, unknown malady, how you make us suffer! I feel now that there are only the two of us. Oh, rich summer night, I now recall the delirious tales that Bacchus told me of his conquest of the Indies! I remember Delphi and can't tear myself away from that memory! Oh, the fury of the shrill flute breaking through the sulfurous storm at the end of a day of harvest calling forth a lustral downpour! Thyrsi and tangled locks. Mysteries of Ceres, mysteries and kermesses, and paupers' graves! . . . Astarte, Ashtaroth! Derceto! Adonai! Let's dance on the meadow still warm from dancing feet with whole boarding schools of Shulamites, to the rousing din of all the Salammbo-ing flutes! Everything is in Everything."

"Don't come near me! What emanates from me is the jealous, nostalgic admiration of happy beings and things for her who, alone and well preserved, makes her way toward the moonlit mountains, for her whose love has many yesterdays but no tomorrows!"

"You are perfect, to be sure, and that armor fits you like a glove. But, poor darling, how will it be in autumn? Won't your heart breathe in the mortality of the landscape so as to make you cough from the depth of your being?"

"I'll curl up in a burrow we have in Hyrcania, and I'll leave it—*Hoyotoho!*—only to eat my fill—*Hoyohei!* of the serene manna of snowfall!"

"Yes, autumn is still a long way off. Perhaps it will never return. And how full the present summer night is! O Syrinx, I can't just go off and leave you! I can't forget you after this day, consoler of my all-encompassing genius! And yet Everything encompasses Everything! And you don't expect me to believe that you are above it all? . . . See, already, those flashes of heat lightning! . . . Astarte! Adonai! It's God's will."

"*Hoyotoho!* Do not come near me! *Heiaha! Heiaha!* Help! . . . Poor boy! . . . Don't you see that pleasure is desire and that happiness comes from passing and making envious those couples laid low by happiness?"

"Very well then. I'll go away and die, but I'd have taken such good care of you! My madness is indeed divine, but not as divine as the prize of your will. Forgive me, and I will die in peace. I'll render up my soul on my elementary, primitive two-penny pipe, playing out the exile with which your vision has honored me."

"But you can see for yourself; there is nothing but art; art is the perpetuation of desire. . ."

Ah, but this time she has spoken in such an equivocally charitable tone that Pan can no longer hesitate. Head lowered, arms spread wide, he advances resolutely toward her! . . . She, poor woman, truly and solely worthy of the name, run down and caught thus on such a beautiful but indifferent evening!

With a supreme burst of inhumanity, with all the immortal virginity of her eyes fixed on him, Syrinx holds Pan back for a second longer, shouts a last *Hoyotoho!* and then throws herself into the light curtain of reeds and drifts off in the water!

And the inspired lover, as he leaps forward, grasps in his sincere arms nothing but the dry plumes of the reeds! He parts them, and gazing down into the water, sees the lovely child rescued by the silent naiads who drag her forward in silent paths, white in their white arms!

All this momentary activity has scarcely ruffled the twilit moiré surface of the stream winding, deathly and slow, under the lovely evening sky.

It has all happened without a word, and it is over.

And evening has come, and sleep will bring no solution. But, oh, is that still her lovely head staring straight out over there on the surface of the water, or just a bunch of water lilies playing about as they do?

It is all over, and the stream slumbers.

This was a real virgin, and the sign of a new era.

Then Pan, being unable to lift his eyes from the tomb of his contradictory dream, from this revelation of a new era for which his genius is perhaps unfit, lets out the "oh" of an adorably youthful melancholic nature. Ah, after this whole day, an "oh" so disinterested, so inviolately inconsolable and unappreciated, so innocently unique. It is one of those "oh's" so delightfully of the kind you just don't hear anymore, no matter what the new era may bring, that as a result a musical voice rises, breathed out from this bunch of water lilies across the way, wafted across the deathly stream, and says: "O breeze, go then and give him back my soul."

And a certain breeze begins to execute gentle rustlings along the curtain of tall hollow reeds, with their long silken leaves and their singing plumes.

What a thing it is, this soul bearing the breeze among the reeds! Pan lifts his pointed ears.

O gentle rustling, winged kisses, flourishes of sound, fans beating together and pulverizing the spray of a fountain deep in the gardens of Armida, crumpled fairy handkerchiefs, silence dreaming aloud, sponge erasing all poetry! . . .

And it mercifully whispers: "Quickly, quickly, my friend, for it is her soul that moves among the reeds that you are holding!"

With both his hands Pan tries to quiet a heart more than ever divine; he wipes away a tear, flings his old pipe into the depth of the stream, and being universally inspired, without a moment's hesitation, without scratching his ear or pulling on his pointed beard, he throws his arms around these enchanted reeds, then cuts three of them into seven gradually decreasing pipes, hollows them out, makes holes in them, and ties them together with two rushes.

And so he has quite a flute, and one of the latest models!

Over it Pan runs his lips, lips parched by thirsting for kisses; and what he draws from it is the miraculous gamut of a new era, naively expressing its fluted happiness, its joy on entering the world on this lovely evening of the Pastoral Age! . . .

Pan, laughing through his tears, turns over and over in his big Caliban fingers, the new flute, the flute with seven pipes, which is the divine Syrinx.

"Oh, thank you, thank you! Seven pipes!"

But it is already dark, and the water lilies that appeared have disappeared.

Pan sits down among the reeds, plays a few opening notes, and then some more, pressing his new toy against his heart, and runs his thick lips along it. Then he meditates.

Night has fallen. Nothing but the loneliness of the countryside can be seen; nothing but the cool flow of the stream can be heard. O memorably attentive night!

Pan begins: "Go over and over the same ground, oh, my song, rather than move forward, just as the terrestrial conscience must if it does not wish to break the charm of Maya, the Comfortable One, and close forever her lovely eyes!"

To begin with, he plays fantastic, throbbing, spasmodic, licentious trills, yelping trills that trail off and die away as if on the pious rosary of some patient on the mend.

Then one isolated and lingering note rises as calm as a balloon above a gaping throng.

And now the song unwinds, yards of it, as wan as a ballad played at a woman's churching, suddenly interrupted by a heavy scale like a bell rung from some hastily constructed scaffolding, then unswathed, unrolled like a garland around a pedestal awaiting a statue that will fortunately never, never come.

And then, pell-mell, come introits as old as the hills, waterless caravans of kyries, marasmic offertories, prayers much the worse for wear, oversimplified litanies, magnificats that go into details, frothy misereres, and stabats sung around a manger or a cistern mirroring Diana-the-Moon.

Pan wipes his lips with the back of his hand, lays down his flute, and says to himself:

"I am all alone: my song is monotonous, for all I can do is love, and since my love has left me I can only sigh until further notice. How this day has flown! Oh, Syrinx, have I dreamt you? I remember her minute by minute, word by word, her glance, the bending of her neck, the tone of her voice; and yet I did not really see her nor hear her! This is another one of those times when I did not have the presence of mind to discover what was really happening! I could have stared at her and listened to her forever and copied her formula right from nature. Instead of which I thought—of what? Of everything? And it's all over. Oh, how incurably part of Everything I am. How careless! Who will now throw up a bridge between my heart and the present! If only she had left a lock of her hair that I could press to my lips to prove that she had been here!"

He takes up his flute with its seven reeds, his talisman, the soul of Syrinx, and puts it to his lips.

And since, on such a beautiful evening of the Pastoral Age, a composer may be permitted to repeat himself, he plays his Stabat again, again on the edge of a font on which rests the image of Diana-the-Moon.

He lifts his eyes; and there is the Moon—a blinding circle, palpable and glorious, climbing, melancholy and pure, above a black line of hills.

Pan dashes through his Stabat and then begins to thunder forth a curse against Diana:

"*Hoyotoho*, up there! O Moon, camphor-colored shield of silence!

"O Diana, your divinity leaves me cold; your physical defects are no business of mine. And why do you go about seemingly equipped with sex? What a disgrace to retain impure organs that are of no use to you! How little immortality there is in a chastity that must, to maintain itself, incur with its charms the revolting and comforting spectacle of a madly enslaved male!

"And how did you come by all this divinity? From some great hidden, impossible love? No, you have never dreamt of our very legitimate sex! No, you were brought up in the forest and knew nothing but hunting the year round and never felt anything softer than a boar's bristles; you heard nothing gentler than the baying of hounds; and you bathed in cold fountains deep in the woods. You are really a man, a proud pale man, a planter with poor white slaves, and you flog your hunting companions, and, with your un-mentionable incantations, cauterize their sex in the claustral tangles of the forest. I know all about you. I am not a madman. Everything is part of Everything, and I am Everything's empirical sentinel."

But the Moon remains there, alone in the sky, a blinding circle. . .

And Pan, who starts to shiver with fever, drifts off into feverish dreams of a Thousand and One Abject Nights, in the evening breeze that saunters along, bearing breaths breathed all over the place, the bleatings of all the folds, the creakings of all the weather vanes, the spicy aroma of all the bandages, the rustling of all the scarves lost among brambles of the highways.

O lunar enchantment! Ecstatic climate! Can this really be? Is this the Annunciation? Or is it just a midsummer night's dream?

And Pan, leaping like a madman, without saying farewell to the still stream and pressing his new flute against his wounded side, gallops off aimlessly through the enchanted night toward his valley, piloted by the moon.

Henceforth, fortunately, during these sorrowful hours all he needs do is blow a nostalgic scale on his Syrinx flute with its seven reeds, open wide his clear eyes, and lift his head toward the Ideal, truly the Master of us all.

PICTURE CREDITS

The frontispiece is a portrait sketch of Laforgue at the Prussian court (1885) by the Croatian painter Franz Skarbina (1849–1910). It is used by permission of M. Jean-Louis Debauve.

The drawings (most of them unpublished) on the title page, and on pages v, vii, 43, 61, 85, 135, and in the section facing page 84 are from Jules Laforgue's Notebook of 1884–85. They are reproduced by permission of the Manuscript Division of the Library of Congress.

The drawing on page 111 is from the collection of Mme Elisabeth van Rysselberghe. It is used by permission of Mme van Rysselberghe and David Arkell. For use of the drawings on pages ix and 5 and for Laforgue's signature on the title page, thanks are due M. Jean-Louis Debauve, the Bibliothèque Littéraire Jacques Doucet, and Professor Warren Ramsey.